# The Palace MURDER

Eliza Thomson Investigates

Book 7

By

VL McBeath

**The Palace Murder**
By VL McBeath

Copyright © 2020 by VL McBeath, Valyn Publishing
(a trading company of Valyn Ltd).

For more about this author please visit:
https://vlmcbeath.com

All rights reserved. No part of this publication may be reproduced, distributed, or transmitted in any form or by any means, including photocopying, recording, or other electronic or mechanical methods, without the prior written permission of the publisher, except in the case of brief quotations embodied in critical reviews and certain other noncommercial uses permitted by copyright law. For permission requests, write to the author at:

https://vlmcbeath.com/contact/

\*

Editing services provided by Susan Cunningham (www.perfectpros-eservices.com)
Cover design: BookCoversbyMelody
(https://bookcoversbymelody.com)

ISBNs:
978-1-913838-06-5 (Ebook Edition)
978-1-913838-07-2 (Paperback)

Main category - FICTION / Historical Mysteries
Other category - FICTION / Crime & Mystery

## Previous book in the *Eliza Thomson Investigates* series

*A Deadly Tonic (A Novella)*
*Murder in Moreton*
*Death of an Honourable Gent*
*Dying for a Garden Party*
*A Scottish Fling*

## Get your FREE copy of *A Deadly Tonic*

by signing up to my no-spam newsletter for further information and exclusive content about the series.

Visit
https://www.subscribepage.com/eti-freeadt

Further details can be found at **www.vlmcbeath.com**

# CHAPTER ONE

*July 1903*

Sergeant Cooper was nowhere to be seen. Eliza shifted her position in the dining room window and peered into the front garden of her friend Connie Appleton. No, he mustn't have arrived. Unless he was early and had gone inside ... but he wouldn't do that. Not yet.

"What are you doing?" Eliza's husband Archie glanced up from his morning newspaper as she pressed her head against the glass.

"I want to know if Sergeant Cooper's arrived at Connie's yet."

"Why should that concern you?"

Eliza spluttered as she turned to face the room. "Why do you think? They're walking out with each other today, for the first time."

Archie folded up the paper and placed it on the table. "I thought they'd been walking out together for months."

Eliza placed her hands on her hips. "Not officially.

Today's a big day for Connie, especially with it being a church outing."

"That still doesn't explain why you're so keen to see him."

"Archie, my dear fellow–" Mr Bell, Eliza's father, winked at her "–how many years ago did you marry my daughter? You should be well aware she likes to know what's going on."

"Exactly." Eliza nodded. "Besides, Connie was rather anxious about the whole thing yesterday; I don't want her to be alone when Sergeant Cooper arrives."

Her son Henry wandered into the dining room and sat next to his grandfather. "You spoilsport. I imagine Sergeant Cooper would like nothing more than to be on his own with Mrs Appleton. He won't want you getting in the way."

"Henry Thomson, you watch your mouth. Connie has a reputation to keep." Eliza peered through the window again. "I'd better go and see her. He could arrive at any minute and she can't invite him in without a chaperone."

Archie rolled his eyes at his son. "Eliza, I'm sure Sergeant Cooper is enough of a gentleman to know he needs to wait outside."

"Maybe you're right, but I can't help worrying about her. You've no idea what this means." Eliza gave another glance up the road before turning to Henry. "Are you sure you won't come with us? I spoke to Mr Hewitt yesterday and there are still a couple of places on the charabanc…"

"No, I told you. It won't be much fun spending the day with a bunch of villagers at least twice my age."

Mr Bell chuckled. "And the rest."

Henry grinned. "I was trying to be polite. Anyway, no, thank you. You go and enjoy yourselves; I've arranged to meet a few of the chaps in The Golden Eagle after luncheon."

"Very well." She hurried to the hall to retrieve her hat before rejoining them and fixing it in front of the mirror over the fireplace. "I'm going to Connie's now. I'd say I'm as nervous as she is."

Henry tutted. "I don't know why; it's not as if she's just met Sergeant Cooper. She's known him for years."

Eliza shook her head as Archie stood up to help her on with her jacket.

"That's beside the point, but never mind, you wouldn't understand." Satisfied that the cream flowers on the rim of her hat set off the green and cream of her suit, she turned back to the table. "I expect we'll be back in five minutes, so can you and Father be ready?"

The morning sun shone down the length of the road as Eliza pulled the front door closed behind her. She gazed at the sky, thankful there were a few clouds. It would get too warm if they disappeared. Adjusting her hat to be sure the rim shaded her face, she hurried next door and gave her usual cursory knock on the door. She was about to let herself in when Connie opened it for her.

"Oh, it's only you." She exhaled deeply.

"And good morning to you too, my dear Connie."

Connie smirked. "You know what I mean, but I'm so nervous about Sergeant Cooper arriving."

"Which is why I came early. Are you ready?"

"Yes, I'd say so. What do you think?" Connie swished the skirt of her lacy white dress.

"You look fabulous." Eliza studied the way Connie's blond hair was swept up onto the top of her head. "I'm so pleased you're wearing that hat as well. The pink suits you."

"I decided it was time to give it an outing. There's no point keeping it in its box."

"Quite right too. Sergeant Cooper will be the proudest man in Moreton having you on his arm."

Connie blushed. "If he ever arrives. You don't think he's forgotten, do you? Or changed his mind?"

"No, I don't; not after all this time." Eliza leaned backwards and peered down the road. "In fact, he's here now, and very smart he is too. I'd say he's had his uniform pressed especially for the occasion."

Connie grabbed Eliza's arm. "I'm so glad you're here. Shall we go out and meet him? I'm not ready to invite him in yet."

Eliza ushered Connie through the open door. "After you."

Sergeant Cooper beamed as Connie stepped towards him. "My word, Mrs Appleton, what a treat you look. And you too, Mrs Thomson; very nice." He smoothed his hands over his uniform.

"You're looking rather trim yourself, Sergeant." Eliza glanced between him and Connie. "You make a lovely couple. Shall we go? We don't want Mr Hewitt wondering where we are."

"Yes, of course. I hope you'll forgive me for being late, but Constable Jenkins wasn't happy about being left at the station while the rest of the village are out for the day." Sergeant Cooper offered Connie his arm.

"I can't say I blame him, but I suppose someone has to stay." Connie's cheeks flushed as she linked her arm through the sergeant's.

"They do indeed. You can never be too careful."

Eliza kept in step with Connie. "We need to call at the

surgery on our way to collect Dr Thomson and my father. They should be ready."

"Right you are." Sergeant Cooper hadn't yet wiped the grin off his face. "What a day this promises to be."

The clock in the bell tower was striking half past nine as they arrived outside the church.

"There's a decent crowd here." Mr Bell studied the sea of faces. "How many are going?"

"About twenty-five I think; I'd say most of them are here."

"They are indeed. Good morning, all." The nasal tones of Mr Hewitt, the churchwarden, pierced the air as he joined them and ticked their names off on his piece of paper. "You couldn't persuade young Henry to join us then?"

Eliza sighed. "No, I'm afraid The Golden Eagle held more interest for him than Hampton Court Palace. I don't know what the world's coming to."

"Don't be too hard on him; I was the same at his age." A wistful look crossed Mr Bell's lined face. "There'll be plenty of time for him to visit the palace when he's older."

Several of the villagers were keen to welcome Dr Thomson on the trip, but everyone stopped and faced the road as two four-horse charabancs drew up beside them.

"Here we are, our carriages await." Mr Hewitt extended his arm towards the first. "Dr and Mrs Thomson, would you care to take a seat while I find the vicar? He's the only one missing."

Concern crossed Connie's face. "That's not like him; he's usually most punctual."

"He's fine, he wanted to nip back into church for something. You all make yourselves comfortable."

The driver stood at the back of the charabanc to help the

ladies climb the steps. Eliza and Connie made their way to the front and sat on one side while Archie, Mr Bell and Sergeant Cooper took seats on the opposite bench.

"Good morning, everyone." Mrs Petty, an elderly neighbour, followed them towards the front of the carriage and sat beside Connie. "May I introduce my friend Mrs Dixon? She's from Over Moreton."

To a chorus of good mornings, Mrs Dixon took the seat opposite her friend.

"Don't they have church outings in Over Moreton?" Connie asked.

Mrs Petty chuckled. "They do, and we go on both. It's very convenient being associated with both churches."

Mr Bell grinned. "I do the same myself. I'm going on a trip to Kew Gardens in a couple of weeks with my church in Richmond."

"Ooh, we've not been there yet. You must tell us what it's like."

"I will. I'm particularly looking forward to seeing the palm house..." Mr Bell paused as a family of four climbed the steps to join them.

"Good morning, Mr King." Archie waved from his seat at the far end. "I didn't think I'd see you here today."

"Why not?" Mr King glared at Archie.

"Well, no reason ... I suppose it's a good opportunity for you to meet the villagers."

"I've a fondness for the palace and haven't been for many years." Mr King's bearded chin jutted forward as he stared straight ahead.

"Ah, right."

"You're new to the village then?" Mr Bell asked. "How are you finding it?"

"As you'd expect. Thankfully, I don't have to work here."

Eliza raised an eyebrow to Archie, but the conversation was cut short when Mr and Mrs Pitt, the local shopkeepers, joined them.

"Do you have room for two more?" Mr Pitt asked.

"We do if we all move up." Sergeant Cooper slid closer to Mr Bell as the ladies similarly squeezed together.

Connie was reluctant to move and kept her voice low as she spoke to Eliza. "I hope this dress doesn't crease."

"It's lace, you'll be fine."

Connie didn't look convinced as she smoothed down the skirt on her knee, but audibly groaned as the vicar and Mr Hewitt climbed aboard.

"If I may ask you to squeeze up a little more." Mr Hewitt chose the more generous space on the predominantly ladies' side. "There we are, right, we're ready to go."

## CHAPTER TWO

The River Thames glistened in the sunshine as the horses trudged across the bridge, but despite straining to catch a glimpse of the palace, Eliza could see nothing but trees.

"We can't be far away. The kings and their courtiers travelled here by boat and we're over the river now."

"Patience, my dear." Mr Bell smiled at his daughter. "We'll be there in a few minutes."

Eliza remained unconvinced as she continued to stare into the distance. "I don't know why I've never been here before. It's only a quarter of an hour's drive from Moreton."

"I blame London and the shops." Archie's soft Scottish accent spoke to no one in particular. "At least it will be more favourable for my wallet coming here."

Eliza suddenly slid forward in her seat. "What's that over there?" She pointed to a turret raising up from behind a bank of trees.

"That's it!" Connie held Eliza's arm. "It must be."

The charabanc followed the road until it turned into a

driveway where an imposing red-brick building stood at the far end. The large gatehouse, sited beneath an impressive oriel window and flanked on either side by towering octagonal turrets, opened up enticingly in front of them.

"Are you sure a day will be long enough to see everything? I'd say it could take all week."

Mr Bell sniggered. "You may be right, especially given the size of the gardens. I was rather hoping we could go to the maze first."

Eliza looked at him. "What do you want to do that for?"

"Well, it's good fun for a start, but it can be quite a squeeze if there are too many people inside. I thought we could walk over there while it's quiet, taking in the grounds as we walk. We'll come back to the house later."

"It sounds like a reasonable plan to me. That way, the palace may be quieter when we get around to it." Archie gave Sergeant Cooper a sideways glance. "Will you and Mrs Appleton join us, Sergeant, or do you have your own plans?"

"I must admit, I haven't given it any thought."

"Oh, please can we go with Dr and Mrs Thomson?" Connie's voice squeaked. "It's always more fun with a group."

"If that's what you'd like, my dear." Sergeant Cooper held her gaze before he faced the rest of the passengers. "Are we all going together?"

"We won't be joining you." Mr King spoke as his wife stared into her lap. "We're here to see the formal gardens, not some silly maze."

"And we'd thought of going into the palace first." Mr Pitt sounded apologetic. "We don't mind missing the gardens, it's the throne room and royal apartments we'd like to see."

Mrs Pitt agreed. "I've already seen the grounds."

Archie smiled. "There's no need to apologise. We don't all have to walk together."

The charabanc suddenly came to a halt outside the main entrance and the driver jumped down to open the door and roll down the steps.

Mr Hewitt was the first out, and he addressed the passengers from the steps. "I hope you all enjoy the day. It's ten o'clock now; may I ask you all to be back by four? If you want to visit the gardens, make your way through the gatehouse and keep walking in a straight line, you'll eventually reach the Fountain Garden. You can then go in either direction to see other places of interest."

Giving no one the chance to ask questions, Mr Hewitt disappeared down the steps and headed to the second charabanc, presumably with the same message.

"I suppose we'd better ask someone else the way to the maze." Eliza watched Mr Hewitt busy himself with the other villagers.

"I'm sure we'll find it. Shall we go?" Archie held out his arm for Eliza, and along with Mr Bell, Connie and Sergeant Cooper, they set off for the gatehouse.

"I reckon it was a good idea to go into the gardens first." Mr Bell pointed to Mr and Mrs Pitt as they joined the queue of people waiting to enter the royal kitchens. "Hopefully all the visitors will arrive this morning and pass through the palace first."

"That would be nice." Eliza smiled at Connie as she walked on the arm of Sergeant Cooper. They'd both lost their tongues, but Eliza had to admit, they made a splendid couple, especially now Sergeant Cooper's portly figure had slimmed down and he'd groomed his moustache. He clearly hadn't wanted to leave anything to chance when wooing Connie.

After dodging the crowds in the Base Court, they passed through the Anne Boleyn Gate into the Clock Court. The crowds had largely dispersed, but a group stood staring at something above the gate.

"What are they looking at?" Eliza followed their gaze. "Is that a clock?"

Mr Bell laughed. "It's rather more than that; it's an astronomical clock."

The line in Eliza's forehead deepened. "It has too many hours?"

"It's a twenty-four-hour clock. The right-hand side shows the times from midnight until noon, and then the numbering starts again for noon to midnight."

"I'd get very confused." Connie appeared as puzzled as Eliza felt.

"What about everything else? I can see the months and the zodiac signs, but I've no idea about the rest."

"You can be forgiven for that, my dear." Archie pointed towards the clock. "If you look at the inner circle, you'll see the number of days since the beginning of the year and the phases of the moon. It would tell the royal bargemen when to expect the low and high tide of the river."

"Well I never!" A smile lit up Sergeant Cooper's face. "It's no wonder we don't have one in Moreton."

Archie chuckled. "No, indeed, but have you seen the time? I think it's showing a quarter past ten; high time we were moving on if we want to keep ahead of the crowds." With a final glance at the clock, he ushered the group towards the arched gateway on the opposite side of the court. "The gardens should be this way. Ah...!"

"What's the matter?" Eliza waited as Archie stepped into a small room that housed an elaborate staircase. "Now where do we go? Mr Hewitt told us to keep straight ahead."

"He did, but obviously not literally." Archie wandered to a door on the far side of the room and disappeared through it. He returned a second later. "It's all right, I think we can go this way."

He stepped back and held open the door while the group filed past him. "It's rather pleasant out there."

Eliza led the way into the corner of a vaulted cloister and squinted as the sun peeped over the top of the state rooms that stood above it. Without waiting for anyone else, she stepped forward to admire the central lawned area containing a large round pool and fountain.

"How splendid." Connie joined her under one of the many elaborate stone archways surrounding the garden. "What a shame we can't wander around. It's lovely and cool in here."

"I'm sure it will be just as nice once we get back." Archie huffed as he checked his pocket watch. "I must have misread the other clock, it's half past ten already, we'd better get a move on."

"So we weren't the only ones who struggled with it." Eliza grinned at Connie as Archie walked on ahead of them.

"It's easy done, it wasn't a straightforward clock." Sergeant Cooper once again took Connie's arm.

"I don't suppose the royal court had much need for precision, back then." Mr Bell strolled behind them with his hands clasped behind his back. "As long as the king was fed on time, he was probably happy."

"I imagine so." Eliza reached out and caught Archie's arm. "Slow down, there's no need to hurry. I'm sure being five minutes late to the maze won't make any difference."

His dark eyes glanced towards her and he struggled to hide a smirk. "You never know."

They walked along the side of the cloister, before turning right.

"I seem to remember there's an entrance to the gardens down here." Mr Bell headed to a door on the left-hand side. "There we are."

He pulled back the door to reveal an entrance lobby that was largely empty. "We're still in good time. If we leave via the door on the other side, we should be in the gardens."

Mr Bell led the way, and within a minute they were on a wide path on the edge of the Great Fountain Garden.

Eliza gasped as she gazed at the enormous pond and fountain situated in the centre of an immaculate semicircular lawn.

"Isn't it fabulous?" Connie's voice was full of awe.

"It is." Eliza took in the view. "And the Kings didn't waste any time getting here." She nodded to a spot close to the fountain. "He must have Mrs King trained well if she's able to walk so quickly."

"I'm sure you could give her a run for her money when the mood takes you." Archie smirked at her. "Not that you seem to be in the mood today. Now, come along. I can see I'm going to have trouble keeping you all moving."

"We'll need to come back another day. We can't possibly

walk around the palace *and* the gardens today. The place must be bigger than Moreton." Eliza turned in a circle. "Which way do we even go for the maze?"

Mr Bell indicated to the left. "If I remember correctly, it's over there, but we can stop and ask, if we see anyone."

They followed the path that ran along the back of the palace until they came to a crossroads. Eliza glanced in all directions. "Now where?"

"There's a man heading towards us in a red tunic. Do you think he works here?" Sergeant Cooper stared towards a path that cut across a less pristine area of grass.

"There's no harm in asking." Mr Bell set off towards the attendant with the rest of the group following him. "Excuse me, sir, is this the way to the maze?"

"Yes, indeed." The man stood with his hands on his hips, then pointed along the path he had just walked down. "If you keep going down here, you run straight into it."

Mr Bell raised his cap. "Thank you, good day."

The attendant continued his stroll and as she watched him leave, Eliza saw Mrs Petty and her friend looking as lost as they had been.

"Over here, Mrs Petty." She waved as her neighbour turned in a full circle.

Mrs Petty gave Eliza a broad grin when she saw her. "Oh, I'm glad we're not the only ones who got lost. Are you still searching for the maze too?"

"We are, although we didn't get lost as such, we've been dawdling." Eliza caught Archie's impatience. "Shall we keep walking?"

"Mrs Dixon and I had a stroll around the Fountain

Garden but then took the wrong path. That's why we're late." Mrs Petty chuckled. "I never did have a good sense of direction."

"Never mind, it's easily done. But we're here now." Eliza followed Archie to the opening. "Can we go in?"

Archie shrugged. "I would say so. After you, Mrs Petty and Mrs Dixon. Perhaps we'll follow you."

Mrs Petty laughed. "Oh, I wouldn't do that if you want to find the centre quickly. I dare say we'll get lost again."

"Maybe we'll take the opposite path then."

Archie and Eliza let the rest of the group enter the maze first and followed them as they headed up the outer edge of the left-hand side. By the time they'd reached the end, there had been no turn-offs, and so they continued to follow the line of the hedge until they were doubling back on themselves.

"Are we sure this is right?" Eliza ran a hand along the hedge. "We haven't missed any openings, have we?"

Archie shook his head. "Not that I've noticed."

"Over here, Eliza." Connie was bouncing on the spot waving an arm. "We have a choice."

Eliza hurried to the opening. "Have you decided which way to go, Mrs Petty?"

"Oh, we don't know, do we, Mrs Dixon? I'll tell you what, we'll keep going straight ahead and you can turn in. I don't want to slow you down."

"As long as you're sure." Mr Bell stepped forward and rounded the hedge to double back on himself. "Just call if you get lost and we'll come and find you."

With a final farewell, Mrs Petty and Mrs Dixon disappeared, leaving the rest of the group to follow Mr Bell deeper into the maze. They hadn't gone far when they hit a dead end.

"Now that's a blow." Sergeant Cooper stopped as Mr Bell turned to face him. "There was another option when we left Mrs Petty; if we go back and take the left fork rather than the right, we should be heading in the right direction."

Mr Bell gave a sigh of resignation. "Very well, Sergeant, lead the way."

They retraced their steps, passing the opening they'd come through, and kept going until they were heading towards the centre of the maze.

"Yes, this feels more like it." Eliza peered through the meagre foliage between a couple of the trees. "I don't think we're near the middle yet, though."

Mr Bell went in front as they followed the path, but suddenly stopped again and groaned.

"Not again." Eliza stood with her hands on her hips. "I've a feeling Mrs Petty chose the right path, after all. Come along, let's follow her."

The new path led them once again to the far end of the maze, and faced with a choice of routes, Archie took the path that appeared to be heading towards the centre.

"This isn't another dead end, is it?" Connie asked as a hedge appeared in front of them.

Archie stepped forward. "No, we're fine, it goes around here. We'll probably end up back where we started, though."

Eliza and Connie giggled, but froze as a shriek filled the air.

Eliza grabbed Archie's arm. "Who on earth's that? And where are they?"

"Is that you, Mrs Thomson?" Mrs Petty's shrill voice filtered through the hedge.

"Mrs Petty, was that you screaming?"

"No, it was Mrs Dixon ... but oh, Mrs Thomson, you need to get here quickly."

Eliza stared at Archie before answering, "What is it?"

"We've found a dead body!"

## CHAPTER THREE

Eliza's heart skipped a beat. "A body!" She spun around on the spot. "How on earth do we get to the centre? We can't do anything here."

Archie put his hands on her shoulders. "Calm down; we'll find a way. Mrs Petty, have you any idea how you got in there so quickly?"

Eliza leaned into the hedge to listen.

"N-no." The tremble in her voice was obvious. "We planned to stick to the perimeter and somehow ended up in the middle."

Archie turned to Sergeant Cooper. "That should help. We were close to the boundary before we came down this track, so I suggest we go back the same way. We came in from the left, so why don't we go right at that junction and see where it takes us?"

"Right you are, Dr Thomson." Sergeant Cooper followed Archie as he shot off towards the back of the maze, abandoning Connie as if he'd forgotten she was with him.

"Wait for me." Eliza chased after them, hoping Connie and Mr Bell would follow her.

When she caught them up, Sergeant Cooper was standing at another junction scratching his head.

"This won't do at all; it isn't the boundary."

"No, it's not." Eliza checked both ways. "Maybe we should turn left here rather than go straight ahead. The boundary must be that way ... I think so, anyway."

Archie ushered her around the hedge. "I'd say you're right."

Within seconds, they were doubling back on themselves, but Eliza squealed when they rounded the next corner. "There it is; you can see the gardens through the hedge. Come along. The middle must be this way."

She hitched up the front of her skirt as she hurried on ahead, pausing only when she met an outcrop of hedge.

"Stick to the outer path." Archie raced past her with Sergeant Cooper in tow. "We must be close."

Seconds later, Eliza turned a corner and ran into the back of Archie and Sergeant Cooper, who had stopped beside Mrs Petty and her friend.

"Oh, Mrs Thomson, you're here." Mrs Petty hurried to Eliza's side. "We were so worried."

Eliza peered into the centre of the maze as she patted the older woman on the shoulder. "Well, we're here now. Why don't you come and stand down here out of the way and let Dr Thomson and Sergeant Cooper deal with things?"

She escorted them away, glancing back along the path she had just run along. "I had expected Mr Bell and Mrs Appleton to be right behind me; they should be here shortly.

If you'll excuse me, I'd like to check whether Dr Thomson needs anything."

Eliza shuddered as she stepped into the open space that was partially shaded by the branches of a young tree, to see a smartly dressed man lying under the right-hand hedge, his bowler hat upside down several feet from his head.

"Is he really dead?" Eliza watched Archie as he knelt beside the body.

"I would say so, although there's no obvious reason why."

Eliza studied the man.

"There are no signs of trauma to his neck or face. Do you know who he is?"

"No, I've never seen him before. What about you, Sergeant Cooper?"

"No, I can't say I have." Sergeant Cooper bent down to check the man's pockets. "Nothing. That won't make things any easier."

"No." Eliza stared down at the limp arms as they splayed out from the body. "Ooh, what's that?"

A trickle of blood appeared from beneath the chest cavity.

Archie leaned over the body. "That might be what we're looking for. Sergeant Cooper, will you help me here?"

The two men turned the body over to reveal a blood-covered wound in the middle of the victim's back.

"Stabbed?" Sergeant Cooper reached for his notepad.

"It would appear so."

"Where's the knife?" Eliza scanned the immediate vicinity as she walked around the hedges that enclosed the centre. "It's not here."

Archie's attention didn't move from the body. "In that case, it could be anywhere."

Sergeant Cooper groaned. "In a place this size too. We'll need an army to do a thorough search."

"And we'll have to search the maze too." Eliza's heart sank. "How will we know where we've searched and where we haven't?"

Archie smirked. "I don't suppose you've a ball of wool in your handbag?"

Eliza gasped. "As if..."

"Mrs Petty may ... or her friend." Sergeant Cooper's face showed no hint of a smile.

"I doubt it."

"There's no harm in asking." Archie glanced up at her.

"I'm not asking them a question like that when they've just found a body."

Archie grunted. "Where are they, anyway?"

"I told them to wait outside. Connie and Father should be with them, as long as they didn't get lost."

Sergeant Cooper's face coloured. "Mrs Appleton; I've gone and left her..."

Eliza smiled. "I'm sure she'll understand; why don't you go and check on her?"

"Yes, I will, thank you."

Archie stood up and smiled at Eliza as Sergeant Cooper scurried away. "You may as well go too. There's nothing much to do here; you'd be better employed finding out if anyone saw anything."

Eliza studied the body. "Should you turn him over again, in case anyone else wanders in?"

"I will, but try to keep them out. I'll stay here for now. In fact, ask Sergeant Cooper to come back, will you? I need him to report this to the palace guards so they can arrange for the body to be taken away. We'll also need someone at the maze entrance to keep everyone out."

Eliza nodded. "I'll speak to Father; he'll be happy to do that, but we need to stop people leaving the grounds too."

"It can't be eleven o'clock yet, nobody will be ready to leave."

"Unless they've committed murder!"

Archie scratched the back of his head. "I suppose you're right; I'll ask Sergeant Cooper to deal with it."

By the time Eliza returned to Mrs Petty, the vicar and Mr Hewitt had joined her, as well as Connie and Mr Bell.

"My, we do have a gathering. I didn't know you were in the maze too, Mr Hewitt."

"We hadn't long been in when Mrs Dixon screamed."

The older woman put a hand to her chest. "I do apologise. It's so undignified, but I got such a shock."

"I think we'd have all done the same thing, and we were grateful you called out, weren't we, Vicar?"

"Indeed. We heard Mrs Petty tell Mrs Thomson to stay near the boundary, and so that's how we arrived here not long after Mr Bell."

Sergeant Cooper poised his pencil over his notepad. "As we're all here, can I ask if anyone spotted anything suspicious? Other than Mrs Dixon, of course."

Eliza leaned over to whisper in his ear. "Actually, Sergeant, Dr Thomson asked if he could have a word with you. He needs your help ... if you wouldn't mind. I'll stay here and ask a few questions. I can update you later."

"Right, yes." Sergeant Cooper surveyed the group. "Excuse me, ladies and gentlemen, I need to go. I'll leave you with Mrs Thomson." He smiled as he walked past Connie. "Will you be all right?"

"Yes, I'll be fine. I'll see you later." Her eyes followed him until he disappeared.

"Do we know who the victim is?" Mr Bell asked.

"Not at the moment." Eliza hesitated as she faced Mrs Dixon and Mrs Petty. "I don't suppose you recognised him?"

"I didn't take much notice if I'm being honest." Mrs Dixon was still shaking. "It was too frightful."

"Me neither." Mrs Petty's face was as pale as Eliza had seen it. "He was just lying there and you could tell…"

"It must have been a terrible shock. Try not to think about it for now and we can talk later."

"Maybe I can help." Mr Bell marched towards the centre of the maze before Eliza could stop him. "He could be someone I know."

"Father, come back."

"I'll only be a minute." Mr Bell squeezed past Sergeant Cooper as he headed in the other direction. "Ah, Archie."

"Mr Bell." Archie scowled at Eliza. "Is he alone? It's not appropriate for everyone to come in here."

Eliza stood by the entrance. "Yes, he is. I'll stay here in case anyone else has the urge to join us."

"So, you don't know who the chap is?" Mr Bell indicated towards the body. "Have you seen his face?"

"Yes, we found him lying on his back. If you'd help me turn him over, you can take a look, but then I want you to go back and join the others."

With the man's face once again visible, Mr Bell studied him. "I must admit, he seems familiar, but I've no idea why."

"It can be difficult once the blood has left the skin."

Mr Bell's eyes narrowed. "I'm sure I know him. This is going to annoy me now until I remember."

"I imagine Sergeant Cooper would like you to remember too." Eliza stepped towards him. "Have you any idea when you may have seen him?"

"No, not a clue, but judging by the age of him, it could have been years ago. Just let me fix his face in my mind and I'll think about it. We can't be hunting for a killer when we don't even know who the victim is."

Archie tapped his foot as he waited. "When you've finished, Mr Bell..."

Mr Bell jolted from his trance. "Yes, I'm sorry."

"We need someone at the entrance to the maze to stop anyone else coming in. Would you do that for us while Eliza speaks to those who are already inside?"

"Yes, of course." Mr Bell regained his urgency. "I'd better go ... and hope no one's joined us in the last ten minutes."

Archie's eyebrows drew together. "At least we got here early. Hopefully, the crowds are still at the house."

Eliza grimaced. "I hope you're right, or this investigation will get very complicated."

By the time Eliza returned, the vicar and Mr Hewitt were consoling Mrs Dixon and Mrs Petty, while Connie stood awkwardly beside them.

"Oh, Eliza, you're here. Isn't this awful? When I was with Sergeant Cooper too. Do you think I'm in the way?"

"Don't be silly." Eliza patted Connie's arm. "Whether you'd come with Sergeant Cooper or not, you'd have been here with me; he's only doing his job. Why don't we pretend it's like old times until we've found the killer, and then you can start again with Sergeant Cooper?"

"You're right; I should know better." Connie's shoulders sagged. "I was just so nervous about today. Did Mr Bell recognise the dead man?"

Eliza shook her head. "No, I'm afraid he didn't. He said he looked familiar but can't place him."

"That's unfortunate." Mr Hewitt had obviously been listening. "Your father knows so many people, he may have met him anywhere."

"Yes, that's the problem." Eliza reached into her bag for her notebook. "Mr Hewitt, you and the vicar arrived at the maze after the rest of us. Did you notice anything suspicious?"

"I'm afraid we didn't; we were talking about it while you were with Dr Thomson. There was no one at the entrance when we arrived, and so we came straight in."

"It sounds as if we all did the same. Did you see anyone on the path outside the maze on your way here? We spoke to an attendant in a red tunic near the house. Was he around when you arrived?"

"I can't say I saw him. Did you, Vicar?"

"No, and I'm sure I would have if he was in red. Which way did you come in? We walked along the kitchen gardens and saw a gardener working, but he was rather involved in what he was doing."

"Oh, we didn't come that way, but you make a good point. We'll speak to the gardeners when we've finished here. They may have spotted something." Eliza made a note in her book. "Once you came inside the maze, did you see anyone then?"

"No, as Mr Hewitt said, we hadn't been in here long before we heard Mrs Dixon call out and made our way here."

"Yes, I'm afraid it's the same for us." Eliza sighed. "I'd

suggest the murderer had been and gone by the time we arrived."

Connie's face paled. "You don't think he's still here, do you? Hiding in one of the dead ends?"

Eliza shuddered. "I hope not, although we walked down enough of them before we got here and we didn't bump into anyone."

"And you can see through some hedges." Mr Hewitt rose onto the balls of his feet. "Even if none of us went down the same track as the killer, we would have noticed him."

"Possibly." Eliza wasn't convinced. "Although I must confess, I wasn't paying much attention."

"Do you think it could be someone who works here then?" Connie asked. "There aren't many visitors in this part of the garden yet."

"There's a good chance it is, but even if we narrow it down to staff, that still leaves us with a lot of people to consider." Eliza slid her notebook back into her handbag. "I'm afraid the investigation's at a dead end before we start. We need to find the murder weapon, as well. It wasn't near the body, so either the murderer still has it, or he disposed of it somewhere in the gardens."

Mr Hewitt and the vicar began walking along the path, their heads down, as they searched for the knife. The ladies looked under the hedges nearer the centre.

"Mr Hewitt, can you come here a minute?" Eliza pointed to a spot of something beneath a gap in the hedge. "What do you think of this?"

"Do you think it's blood?" Connie asked.

"It could be. I'll have to get Archie to check it, but I wonder if it means the knife's around here."

Mr Hewitt crouched down to inspect it. "It's blood all right, but there's no weapon."

"Let me get Dr Thomson." Eliza hurried back to Archie, who was still with the body. "We think there's some blood out here, will you come and take a look?"

Archie followed Eliza to the hedge. "It's definitely blood, but how did it get here?" He examined a gap in the hedge immediately above the spot. "Would you say this is big enough for someone to squeeze through? When we arrived, the victim hadn't been dead for long, and so maybe the murderer waited until the coast was clear and climbed out here. I'd suggest it leads back to the entrance, and it would explain why nobody saw him."

"It must have been somebody small." Connie studied the opening. "There isn't much of a gap."

"It may be bigger than you think." Archie stood up and pushed his leg through, pulling back the branches that covered the opening. "See how they move and then spring back when I take my leg out."

"So you reckon the murderer watched us all come in and then made his escape when we moved to the other end of the maze?" Eliza had her notebook out again.

"I'm not saying that's what definitely happened, but it's a possibility."

Eliza reread her notes before she put her book away. "We can't do much more here. Mr Hewitt, will you escort Mrs Petty and Mrs Dixon back to the palace and find them a cup of tea? Dr Thomson needs to wait with the body, and I'd like to talk to the gardeners with Mrs Appleton. We'll follow you as soon as we can."

"I think we can manage that."

"On the way out, will you keep your eyes open for the knife? We can't be certain the killer left through this gap."

"Even if he did, he could have thrown it over the hedges," Connie said.

"Yes, indeed." Eliza scanned the surrounding trees. "I'd suggest we all go carefully as we leave, in case the killer's still with us... And you be careful too, Archie."

## CHAPTER FOUR

With only one wrong turn, the group reached the exit to find Mr Bell in discussion with a number of visitors.

"I'm sorry, it's not possible to go into the maze at the moment. Try again this afternoon."

With a lot of muttering, the guests left, and Eliza sidled up behind her father.

"Have you had to turn many away?"

"No, not yet, but it's only likely to get worse. We could do with finding that attendant we spoke to earlier. He'd be more officious."

"You're right, he would." Eliza's eyes searched the path that ran the length of the maze. "He doesn't seem to be here, but that red tunic should help us find him."

The rest of the group were still hovering near the entrance, and Eliza caught Mr Hewitt's attention.

"The house is back down there. Would you mind keeping an eye out for a man in a red tunic as you go and ask him to come here to relieve my father? You remember him, don't you, Mrs Petty?"

"He was difficult to miss, dressed as he was."

"Exactly. The thing is, we really need someone with more authority to stop people entering the maze."

"Consider it done." Mr Hewitt raised his hat to them. "I'll see you later."

Eliza waited for them to leave. "Right, that's all that sorted out. Connie and I will go to the kitchen garden; if we find the attendant on our way, we'll send him over."

Mr Bell positioned himself in front of the entrance. "I can manage for now, and I'll keep Archie company once the other chap gets here. The vicar and Mr Hewitt don't need me joining them."

Seeing the twinkle in his eye, Eliza bid him farewell and linked her arm into Connie's. "Let's see if we can find the gardeners."

They hadn't gone more than ten steps when Connie pointed to a gardener halfway down the outside edge of the maze. "Who's that?"

Eliza raised an eyebrow at the sight of an elderly man attacking the hedge with a pair of shears. "Shall we go and ask?"

They stepped off the footpath and picked their way across the grass until they drew level with the man, who had tufts of grey hair protruding from the edges of his cap.

"Good morning, sir." Eliza used her cheeriest voice, but he did nothing but stare at her. "I wonder if you can help us. There's been a bit of an *incident* in the maze, and we'd like to ask if you've seen anyone go in or out of it in the last hour or so."

"Who are you?"

Eliza forced a smile. "Forgive me, my name is Mrs Thomson, and this is Mrs Appleton. My husband is a local doctor and we're helping the police with their enquiries into the incident I mentioned."

"The police?"

Eliza nodded, her expression grave. "Yes, unfortunately we've had to enlist their services, but at the moment, Sergeant Cooper's gone to alert the guards, and so we offered to talk to anyone in or near the maze."

"I see." The gardener's attention flitted around the grounds while Eliza took out her notebook.

"May I take your name?"

"Well ... I suppose. It's Boyle. Mr Boyle. Head gardener."

"So, Mr Boyle, may I ask how long you've been here?"

He gestured to the hedge behind him. "I've trimmed most of this side; I was here before the place opened this morning."

Eliza turned to study the view. "By the looks of it, the entrance to the maze isn't visible from here; did you see anything while you were near the footpath?"

"I started at the back and haven't been beyond here."

Eliza pointed to a small patch that had been clipped at the front of the hedge. "Did you start near the path?"

"Oh, that was nothing. I wanted to be sure the shears were working, so I tested them on that small area. As soon as I knew they were sharp, I moved to the back."

"And did you notice anyone going into the maze while you were still on the footpath?"

Mr Boyle shook his head. "I didn't see anyone, although once I was working near the back, I did hear a few voices. And someone screaming."

"So you heard that. We're particularly interested in the half an hour before the scream. Did you see anyone walking along the path towards the maze?"

"Now you mention it, there were a number of people, not that I knew any of them. One was a vicar who arrived with another man. Then there was a smartly dressed gentleman…"

Eliza's head jerked up. "Could you give us any more details about him? His height, hair colour, that sort of thing."

"Not really. His hair was hidden under his bowler hat, but I'd say he was taller than the average gent. It's difficult to tell from a distance."

"What time was this?"

Mr Boyle shrugged. "Half an hour, an hour ago? I was nearer the far end of the hedge at the time."

"And was he with anyone?"

"No, he was on his own, looking as pleased as punch."

Eliza made a note in her book. "That's interesting, did you see anyone else?"

"There was another man, maybe five minutes later. He was tall too, bigger than the first, and he had a dark beard."

Eliza examined the footpaths. "And he would have come from the gardens to the right of here?"

"Aye. He was in a hurry, now I come to think about it."

Eliza paused to study her notes. "And there was no one else here?"

Mr Boyle shook his head. "Only Mr Turner, one of our gardeners. He was pottering around."

"Was that before or after you saw the other two?"

Mr Boyle puffed out his cheeks. "Now you're asking. I wasn't paying much attention, to be honest. He's here so often…"

"Yes, of course. Could you tell me where Mr Turner's working? We'll need to talk to him."

Mr Boyle wagged his finger at them. "Don't you go stopping him doing his job."

"I promise we won't take up any more time than we need to. Thank you, Mr Boyle."

Connie led the way back to the path. "Where are we going now? Mr Boyle didn't actually tell us where to find Mr Turner."

"Good point. I assumed he'd be in the kitchen gardens, given that was where we were going; if he's not, we'll have to ask."

Once they were back on the path, Eliza spotted the man with the red tunic standing beside her father. "Look who's there. Why don't we go and ask the attendant where we'll find Mr Turner? He won't be worried about us disturbing his work."

Mr Bell smiled at the ladies as they rejoined him. "I wasn't expecting you back so soon."

Eliza indicated to the attendant. "We were heading over to the kitchen gardens when we saw you had someone to take over from you. We also hoped this gentleman might be able to help us."

The man in the tunic saluted. "Good morning, ladies. Mr Marshall at your service. How may I help you?"

"You're the gentleman who directed us to the maze, I believe."

"Yes, indeed. I never forget a pretty lady ... or two." He laughed at his own joke. "Mr Bell's told me of the *problem*."

"That's good. Has he asked if there was anyone else here before we arrived?"

Mr Bell cleared his throat. "I was getting to it."

"It's as well we came back then. Mr Marshall, did you see anyone?"

"Mr Bell has given me a description of the *victim*, and I must admit, I watched him heading here from the kitchen gardens."

"Do you know when that was in relation to when we arrived?"

"Well now, I was walking around these parts, waiting for the visitors to arrive, and he came from the far corner…" He pointed down the path, beyond the maze towards the kitchen garden. "I walked towards him and said '*Good Morning*' as we crossed. I carried on to the nearest garden and then headed towards the palace."

"And is that when you met us?"

"No, not that time. I must have walked for another five minutes or so, then I saw another man heading towards me from the same direction as the first."

"Can you describe him?"

"Now, let me think. He was taller than average, if I'm not mistaken, and had a dark beard, although it may have been speckled with grey. He walked with some authority; in quite a hurry he was too."

*That's interesting.* Eliza wrote in her notebook. "Do you know if he went into the maze?"

"Now, I can't say for certain. He'd already walked past by the time I saw him and was heading to the palace. Or at least that's where I thought he was going. It turned out he was going to the Fountain Garden."

"You stood and watched him?"

"No, not at all. Visitors may have needed me and so I

continued my walk, but when I returned to the path near the palace, he was running over the grass towards a woman and two children."

"He shouldn't have been on those lovely lawns." Connie's voice squeaked.

"Exactly, Miss. That was why I noticed him. If I'd been closer, I'd have given him what for; but you can't go shouting around here."

"No, I'm sure you can't." Eliza suppressed a smile. "Did you see anyone else, Mr Marshall?"

"No, I can't say I did. We were quiet until you arrived."

"Well, thank you, anyway. You've been very helpful. May I ask one last question? We were told that one of your gardeners, a Mr Turner, was in the area at the time. Would you know where we might find him?"

Mr Marshall's brow furrowed. "I don't remember seeing him. Was he in the maze?"

"That's what we'd like to ask, if you could tell us where he is."

## CHAPTER FIVE

Eliza and Connie bid Mr Marshall farewell and headed off towards the kitchen gardens. The ground crunched underfoot as they walked, and Eliza waited until they were out of earshot before she gave Connie a sideways glance.

"Did you spot anything when we were talking to Mr Marshall and Mr Boyle?"

"What like?"

"Like the fact that they both mentioned there was a man in a hurry..."

"Yes, they did." Connie's voice was shrill. "One saw him heading towards the maze and the other saw him leaving."

"Except, we can't be sure he actually went in."

"No." Connie's forehead creased. "It will be difficult to find out as well if we don't know who he is."

"But we might..."

Connie's eyes narrowed. "What do you mean? You couldn't possibly recognise him from such a general description."

"I'm not sure that I do, but did you recognise anyone when they described him?"

"Well, yes. They said he was tall with a dark beard, although that's not much to go on."

"No, it's not, but as they were talking, one man sprang to mind; especially when Mr Marshall said the beard may have been going grey and he'd seen him running across the grass towards a woman and two children."

"It's still not much to go on. Plenty of men have grey beards and families."

Eliza stared at some greenhouses in the distance. *Maybe I'm reading too much into this.*

"What's the matter. Do you know who it is?"

"I can't be sure. We didn't see many men when we walked to the maze, but a tall man with a beard and a family accompanied us on the charabanc."

"Mr King!" Connie stopped. "You don't think..."

"I don't know, but is it too much of a coincidence?"

"Oh, I hope it is. I don't want there to be a murderer living in Moreton."

"No, me neither." Eliza sighed. "Come on, let's not worry about it for now. We're almost at the kitchen gardens, and we need to treat the gardeners as suspects, given they could all find their way in and out of the maze."

"Of course, I hadn't thought of that. Do you think even Mr Boyle could be a suspect?"

Eliza cocked her head to one side. "I'm sure he could be, but he'd cut quite a lot of that hedge. We could do with checking he did it all this morning."

"Mr Marshall should know, if he was walking up and down the main path."

"He should." Eliza reached into her bag for her notebook. "I'll make a note to ask him; this Mr Turner may have seen him too."

A man appeared from behind a row of tall shrubs causing Connie to grab for Eliza's arm.

"Did someone mention my name?"

Eliza's lips curved into a smile as a slim, dark-haired man stood in front of her. "Mr Turner?"

"That's me."

"Ah, splendid. Mr Marshall suggested we'd find you here."

Mr Turner's forehead creased. "Mr Marshall? Why were you asking him?"

"There's been an incident in the maze and we're helping the police; I'm Mrs Thomson and this is Mrs Appleton."

The puzzled expression remained on the gardener's face.

"We're looking for anyone who was in the area between ten and eleven o'clock, and Mr Boyle said you were over there."

Mr Turner's eyes narrowed further. "What sort of incident?"

"I'd rather not say at the moment." Eliza smoothed her hand over her notebook. "Can you tell us what you were doing there?"

"Nothing!" He took a step back from them. "I'd left my shears and needed to pick them up."

"And did you notice anyone while you were there?"

"No. I was there and back too quickly."

Eliza's pencil scratched the page as she wrote. "So, you didn't see Mr Boyle cutting the hedge?"

"Well, yes, now you mention it, I did, but that was as I

walked towards the maze. I didn't see anyone while I was there."

"Could you tell us which part of the hedge he was cutting?"

Mr Turner screwed up his face. "He wasn't near the footpath, he was closer to the back, I would say."

"Splendid." Eliza smiled. "And what time was that?"

Mr Turner shrugged. "I couldn't say for sure. The gardens must have been open because there were visitors walking around..."

"So there were other people?"

"Of course ... but not when I was at the maze. That was when I was here ... after I'd walked back."

Eliza pursed her lips as she continued writing. "Could you describe any of them?"

"Now, let me think. There was one man who was very smartly dressed. He wore a suit that looked expensive ... and a bowler hat." He touched his own cap while glancing at his dirty overalls. "And he had a purposeful stride too." He released a deep sigh as if pleased with himself.

"Was there anyone else?"

"Yes. There was another man, who seemed rather out of place. He was almost running when he came down here." Mr Turner motioned towards the path that led to the maze. "He was tall with dark hair and a greying beard."

Eliza glanced up. "Did either man go into the maze?"

Mr Turner nodded. "They both did. I had a good view from where I was working and at a guess, I'd say the first man was about five minutes ahead of the second. The second man wasn't in the maze long before he left." His brow furrowed as he gazed at a spot above Eliza's head. "Now I think about it, I didn't see the other man leave."

"No, you wouldn't. Unfortunately, he's been found murdered."

"Murdered!" Mr Turner dropped his spade. "Good grief. And you think this second man did it?"

"It's too early to say that at the moment, but we'd certainly like to speak to him. Did you recognise him, or the first man, by any chance?"

Mr Turner sucked air between his teeth. "No, I can't say I did. I'd probably remember the second man if I saw him again, though. I'll watch out for him if you like."

"That would be helpful." Eliza was about to close her notebook when she stopped. "One more question. How long after you'd left the maze did this happen?"

"It can't have been long because I hadn't started work properly; I was still sorting out my tools. You can ask Mr Clark." Mr Turner waved to another gardener working on the far side of the plot.

"Thank you, we will. In fact, will you join us?"

Mr Turner hesitated before escorting them to a border full of trellis supporting pea and bean plants. "Mr Clark, do you have a minute?"

The older man straightened up his back. "What can I do for you?"

Mr Turner gestured towards Eliza and Connie. "These ladies are looking for a murderer and I want them to be sure it wasn't me."

Mr Clark's mouth fell open as he gaped at the group. "M-murder?"

Eliza grimaced. "Unfortunately, yes. In the maze."

"I told them I nipped over there to get my shears, but I was here for the rest of the time." Mr Turner gabbled his words. "You've seen me working here all morning, haven't you?"

"Yes, we were here together the whole time." The gardener's face was earnest as he gazed around the garden.

"So you can give each other an alibi?"

They both nodded as Eliza continued. "May I ask if you saw anyone walking past here on the way to the maze?"

Mr Clark's watery eyes searched Mr Turner's face. "Erm, no, but I had my back to the path for most of the morning, so I mustn't have noticed."

"But you saw Mr Turner disappear for a few minutes?"

Mr Clark paused, as if deciding how to answer. "He wasn't here when I arrived, but he was back within a minute."

"Thank you both." Eliza surveyed the rest of the gardens. "Are there any other gardeners around here we can talk to?"

Mr Turner shook his head. "No, there are probably a couple in the walled gardens, but they won't have seen anything."

"Very well, thank you." Eliza turned to leave but immediately stopped. "Where does this path lead?" She pointed to the path the men had walked along.

"If you go to the right, it will take you back to the main entrance."

Eliza raised an eyebrow. "So, we don't need to walk through the palace?"

Mr Turner laughed. "Gracious, no. We'd get nothing done if we had to do that. If you turn left, it takes you around the maze and onto the Lion Gate."

"The Lion Gate?"

"Yes, it's the way most of the locals come in. It saves them having to go all the way around the river."

Eliza linked her arm through Connie's. "I suggest we wander over there on our way back to the main entrance."

Within five minutes, the imposing pillars of an ornate, wrought-iron gate, topped with sculptures of lions, came into view. Eliza hurried towards them.

"These are still open."

Connie gasped. "I imagine Sergeant Cooper knows nothing about them."

"No, I don't suppose he does." She spun around on the spot. "At least there are not many people around, but that's beside the point. The murderer could have easily left this way before we'd even found the body. Come along, we'd better get back to the main entrance and tell him."

They hurried back past the gardeners, who were deep in conversation, before they reached a small wooden gate on the side of the house. Eliza clicked on the latch and pushed the gate open.

"We're here already!" She stood beside the front wing of the palace, staring out over the main driveway. "That was significantly quicker than the way we walked to the maze. I wonder why Mr Hewitt told us to go the way he did."

Connie put a hand to her mouth. "You don't think he did it on purpose to get us out of the way, do you?"

Eliza's stomach flipped. "Oh my, I hope not. Surely he wouldn't do anything underhand if he had the vicar with him?"

"You're right." Connie paused. "Maybe he didn't know he was doing anything wrong. Mr King, if that's who it was in the maze, may have asked him to keep this path clear."

THE PALACE MURDER

"Would he do that with Mr Hewitt? I'm not sure they're that friendly." Eliza reached for her notebook once more. "We'd better check, though. It's a good job I always carry this with me; I'll need a new one at this rate."

Sergeant Cooper was in discussion with a group of police officers when they arrived. At the sound of them approaching, he stopped what he was doing and gave them a broad grin. "Ladies."

"Good afternoon, Sergeant Cooper." Eliza returned his smile. "Have you had to stop anyone from leaving yet?"

"No, I can't say we have. I've been updating the local lads here about what's been going on."

"Have they told you about the Lion Gate?" Connie's face was pained as she gabbled her words.

"The Lion Gate?"

"I presume that's a no, then." Eliza sighed as she glanced at a group of nearby police officers. "It's another entrance over by the maze. Can you send a couple of men over there as quickly as possible? The killer could have gone out that way."

"Right you are, Mrs Thomson." Sergeant Cooper strode over to the group. "Constable. I need you and one of your colleagues over by the Lion Gate now. Why didn't anyone tell me there was another entrance and exit?"

The young constables looked at each other.

"Sorry, Sarge, we thought you knew."

"How would I...?"

The constables didn't wait for the rest of the answer. "We'll be there in five minutes, Sarge. See you later."

Sergeant Cooper took a large white handkerchief from his pocket and wiped his brow. "These youngsters..." His cheeks flushed as Connie smiled at him.

"You weren't to know. How have you been getting on here otherwise?"

The sergeant suddenly puffed out his chest again. "Very well, actually. We've closed off the gate to people coming in and out; I've a couple of men checking the maze more thoroughly for the murder weapon; and I've wired a telegram to New Scotland Yard asking for an inspector to join us."

"Oh, well done." Connie was about to clap her hands in front of her chest, but appeared to have second thoughts.

"Did you ask for Inspector Adams?" Eliza asked. "It's so much easier working with someone we know."

The sergeant's smile didn't falter. "It is, and I did. Hopefully, he'll be here sometime this afternoon. Did you find out anything from the gardeners?"

"We did, as it happens, and a statement from Mr Marshall, the garden attendant, agrees with what they told us. Two men were seen entering the maze at about the right time. One matches the description of the dead man, but the other ... well, his description could be one of our own villagers."

"Mrs Thomson, you can't go around making accusations about innocent men…"

"Sergeant, I'm well aware of that, and it's possible that there are two men of similar appearance, but we need to be watching out for a tall man, with dark, greying hair and a beard. He was with a woman and two children. Does that match anyone you've seen today?"

"I suppose now you mention the villagers, it does match the description of Mr King."

Eliza smiled. "That was my thought. Now, I'm not saying he's guilty, but he has to be a suspect. Especially as he was probably in the maze at the time the man was murdered."

## CHAPTER SIX

Eliza and Connie wandered to the shade of the gatehouse while Sergeant Cooper continued to instruct the local police, who were hoping to find the murder weapon.

"The problem is, it could be anywhere." Eliza glanced back along the path. "If you were the murderer, where would you throw it?"

Connie scowled. "If it was me, I'd probably pop it in my handbag and get as far away from here as possible."

"Ah, that's a woman's logic, but a man wouldn't do that, especially not if they work here."

"So you think it's a man?"

"Oh, goodness, yes. Don't you?"

"What do you want Mrs Appleton to agree with now?"

Eliza swung around to see Archie smiling at her, Mr Bell by his side.

"I don't want her to agree with anything, I'm asking her opinion about the murderer. Would you say it's a man?"

Archie shrugged. "You can never be certain, but I imagine

it was. Did any of the witnesses report seeing a woman near the maze, besides the ladies in our party?"

"No, they didn't, but there's one man who was seen by everyone."

Mr Bell grunted. "Sounds fishy to me. It's unusual for everyone to be in agreement. If it's true, he'll need a solid alibi."

"That's a good point." Eliza turned to Archie. "Do you think we should be suspicious of so many sightings?"

"You mean that all the witnesses are in on the murder and they're trying to pin the blame on someone else?" Archie grimaced. "It's a possibility, I suppose."

"Perhaps we should identify and talk to the man in question." Eliza paused at the sound of footsteps and turned to see Mr and Mrs Pitt walk up beside them.

"We're not late, are we?" Mrs Pitt asked. "We didn't think we were meeting until four o'clock."

"No, not at all." Eliza put on her best smile. "It's just that there's been an incident in the maze, and we're here to find out how Sergeant Cooper's getting on."

"What sort of incident?" Mr Pitt put a protective arm around his wife.

"Well–" Eliza hesitated "–I'm afraid to say that a man's been murdered..."

"Murdered!" The colour drained from Mrs Pitt's face.

"Surely there's been some mistake." Mr Pitt's head spun around to face Archie. "Dr Thomson, are you aware of this?"

"Unfortunately, I am, and we're waiting for an inspector from New Scotland Yard to arrive..."

As if on cue, an official-looking carriage rounded the corner and pulled into the drive.

"This could be him." Eliza took Archie's arm. "Will you excuse us?"

Connie and Mr Bell followed Eliza's lead and waited with Sergeant Cooper as the horses came to a halt. There was silence as the door opened and the inspector and one of his sergeants stepped out.

"Inspector Adams!" Eliza's face broke into a grin as he placed his familiar grey trilby on his greased black hair. "We were hoping it would be you!"

The inspector laughed. "Mrs Thomson; I bet you were." He shook hands with Sergeant Cooper, Archie and Mr Bell. "It's good to see you all again ... although obviously not under the circumstances. How are you all?"

"We're fine, thank you." Eliza smiled. "I hope you are too."

"I mustn't grumble." He rubbed his hands together. "Now, what do we have here?"

Eliza grimaced. "How much did Sergeant Cooper tell you about the murder?"

"Only that you'd found a body in the maze. Do we know who the dead man is yet?"

"No, sir." Sergeant Cooper stood to attention. "He had no papers about him."

Mr Bell coughed to clear his throat. "I've a feeling I recognise him, but I can't work out where from."

Inspector Adams retrieved his notepad. "That could make things difficult. What about the murder weapon?"

"We know it was a knife, but it wasn't with the body. We searched the obvious places, without success. Other than that, it's a rather large space." Sergeant Cooper gestured around the grounds with his arm.

The inspector's eyes flicked across the front of the building. "Any suspects?"

"There were a couple of people near the maze at the time." Eliza consulted her notes. "One was a gardener who says he was only there to pick up some shears; the other is a man we've not been able to track down."

Inspector Adams lifted an eyebrow. "Tell me more."

"Well, the murdered man was seen approaching the maze, probably between quarter past and half past ten, and about five minutes later a tall man with dark, greying hair and a beard followed him in. A man of a similar description was later spotted joining a woman and two children."

Sergeant Cooper interrupted. "It's possible the man who joined the family is one of our villagers."

Inspector Adams glared at the sergeant. "Why hasn't he been arrested then?"

"Unfortunately, nobody's seen him since the sighting in the Fountain Garden. We've been expecting him to try to leave the premises, but so far he hasn't. We've certainly not seen a family of four. We'll keep a lookout for them, sir."

"Very well. Now, I need to see the murder scene. Sergeant, you come with me; Dr Thomson, I'll catch up with you later. Enjoy the rest of your day if you can."

Eliza pursed her lips as Sergeant Cooper attempted to wave to Connie without Inspector Adams seeing him. He may have succeeded had Connie not waved back at precisely the moment the inspector turned around, causing her cheeks to colour. With a low gasp, she grabbed Eliza's arm.

"Oh my goodness, he saw me. I suspect he doesn't know we're walking out together."

"It's nothing to be ashamed of, you're entitled to spend time together if you want to."

"But what will he think?"

Eliza patted her on the shoulder. "He'll think that Sergeant Cooper's a very lucky man, now stop worrying."

"I hope you're right." Connie took a deep breath. "Look, Mr and Mrs Pitt are by the gatehouse with Mrs Petty and Mr Hewitt. Shall we join them?"

"I really don't think I want to. Could we walk by ourselves for a while to mull over what we know? I'm not ready to answer questions at the moment."

"Why don't we go towards the Pond Garden then?" Mr Bell suggested. "It's in the opposite direction to the maze and is supposed to be full of exotic and rare plants. You'll probably enjoy it."

The red-brick facade of the south-facing wing loomed ahead of them, and Eliza shielded her eyes as the sun glistened on the river on the other side of the boundary.

"It's such a lovely place."

"It is, especially on a day like today." Mr Bell walked beside Connie. "You can almost imagine a flotilla of royal barges sailing up the river. They'd probably have disembarked about here."

"Really?" Connie's voice was breathless. "What a shame Sergeant Cooper isn't here to see it."

"There'll be another time. For now, he'll have to make do with you telling him about it." Eliza stopped as they entered the Pond Garden. "Look at that. It must have taken months to dig out so much earth."

"Either that, or a lot of men." Archie scowled as he

studied the sunken flower beds. "I don't suppose King Henry wanted to wait."

Mr Bell rubbed a hand on his chin. "I've a feeling he initially had the earth dug out to make fish ponds. Can you imagine that? It was Queen Mary who planted them again."

"Well, whoever it was, they did a marvellous job." Eliza admired the straight lines of the flower beds. "They must have dozens of gardeners working here to keep the place so tidy."

"They're not that tidy." Connie pointed to the bottom of a flight of stone steps. "Look at that dirty rag, it should be in a litter bin, it spoils the whole effect of that entire border." She bent down to pick it up but immediately dropped it again. "There's something in it."

Eliza watched as Archie stepped towards it and tugged on the cloth. As the blood-stained material unravelled, a well-worn knife fell to the ground with a thud.

"The murder weapon?" Eliza stared at it from her position on the footpath.

"I would say so. We'd better take it to Inspector Adams, and I'll need to check it against the wound, but I can't think of another reason for it being here."

"We'll have to mark where we found it." Eliza scanned the rest of the path. "I wonder how it got here."

Connie's forehead creased. "Mr Marshall said that the man matching Mr King's description ran across the lawns of the Fountain Garden. Maybe he came here first and threw the knife away."

Eliza's eyes narrowed. "It's a long way from the maze. If he was the murderer, it wouldn't have been easy for him to get here."

"It might not have been too bad if he came along the

shortcut, like we did. He'd only have to cross the front drive to get here, and then he could have carried on and joined the family." Connie gazed out across the gardens.

"It's possible, but it would be quite a diversion." Mr Bell walked back to the corner of the palace. "Besides, it would have taken him through the crowds at the entrance."

Eliza sucked the end of her pencil. "What if he went to the Fountain Garden first to meet the family and then brought them around here on their way to the main entrance?"

"But Sergeant Cooper said they hadn't seen a family trying to leave." Connie's cheeks flushed once more as she mentioned the sergeant.

Eliza groaned. "Sergeant Cooper didn't get here immediately, did he? He was at the maze with us for at least ten minutes after we'd found the body. That would have given the murderer time to escape."

"That wasn't his fault though."

"No, of course it wasn't, but it does mean we have to find Mr King as soon as we can, even if it's only to confirm he had nothing to do with it."

"You're right, but we can't do anything about it here." Archie wrapped the knife in his clean handkerchief. "We need to get this to Inspector Adams and then leave it to him."

"But we can help." Eliza hurried beside Archie as he strode back towards the palace. "Inspector Adams doesn't know what Mr King looks like. We do."

"And so does Sergeant Cooper." Archie continued walking until he reached the barrier the police had erected. "Now, where's Inspector Adams?"

"Didn't he go to the maze with Sergeant Cooper?" Connie scanned the driveway.

"Goodness, yes. I'd forgotten. What do we do now?" Archie paused and took out his pocket watch. "It's just turned three o'clock. We've probably got time to go over and find him if you like."

Eliza pursed her lips. "We could, but the knife's clearly old, and I wouldn't be surprised if it came from the palace kitchens. Might we be better going to the main kitchen ourselves to ask if they've lost a knife?"

"It makes sense, besides we wanted to visit the kitchens." Mr Bell winked at his daughter. "We need to turn to the left once we're through the gatehouse. Hopefully, the crowds will have gone."

"Very well." Archie slipped his watch back into the pocket of his waistcoat. "Follow me."

The Fish Court leading to the Great Kitchen was empty as they walked through, and only a handful of visitors admired the large open fireplaces to the left-hand side of the enormous space. Eliza's eyes flicked around the room, finally resting on a group of staff congregated around a wooden table.

"May I help you, sir?" A young man in Tudor costume stepped forward to greet Archie.

"Yes, indeed. My name's Thomson, Dr Thomson, and I'm here on behalf of the police. I presume you've seen them on the front driveway."

"We have that, sir. You wouldn't know what's going on, would you?"

Archie shook his head. "If they've not yet given any details, then I'm probably not at liberty to say, but may I ask if you're missing a knife in here?"

The man turned back to his fellow workers, but they were already no more than two paces behind him. "Not that I'm aware of, but we do have a number of knives and we'd need to count them."

"How often do you count them?"

The young man seemed surprised to hear Eliza speak. "We don't."

"So do you have any idea how many knives there should be?"

There was a collective shake of heads.

"Very well." Eliza nodded to the package in Archie's hand. "May we show them?"

Archie stepped towards the table and, with a flourish, unwrapped the cloth. "We happened to find this knife out in the gardens no more than half an hour ago and wondered if it might have come from here." He had paused to scan the faces of those watching when an elderly man, dressed to imitate a chef, spoke up.

"I was looking for that earlier. Where did you get it from?" He reached down to pick up the knife, but Archie put out a hand to stop him.

"I'm afraid we need to keep it for the time being and pass it to the police. I'm sure they'll send it back once they've finished with it."

"But that's my best meat knife."

"I'm sorry, sir, but thank you for confirming it came from here." Eliza smiled. "Can you tell us where you were this morning?"

The man's brow creased. "Me? Why? I was in here all the time. Didn't leave the place once."

Eliza glanced at the group surrounding him. "And these

men can confirm that?"

"Yes, of course. What's this all about?"

Eliza ignored the question. "Would you care to tell us how this knife ended up in the Pond Garden?"

"No ... I didn't take it. None of us did."

"You can vouch for them all?" Eliza searched the face of each man in the group.

"Yes, we're all here while the visitors are around."

Eliza sighed. "Very well. One last thing. Did you notice any of the guests taking a special interest in the knives? A man with dark hair and a beard, for example?"

The same man replied. "I didn't, that's why I was searching for it. I wasted a good ten minutes, if you must know."

When the others in the kitchen confirmed that they'd seen no one acting suspiciously, Eliza turned to Archie. "I suppose we'd better go and see if Inspector Adams is back. We need to give him the knife, and he may want to come to the kitchen himself."

## CHAPTER SEVEN

It was approaching five to four when they left the kitchen and hurried back to the gatehouse, hoping Archie's pocket watch wasn't running slow. Eliza gave a sigh of relief when they were met by Mr Hewitt ready to mark them present on his piece of paper.

"Ah, here you are." He crossed their four names from his list. "Have you seen Inspector Adams? He was looking for you."

"No, not yet, but he's down there." Archie gestured towards the barrier the police had erected. "We need to talk to him before we leave."

Without waiting for approval, Archie led the group down the driveway.

"I hope they have as many people on the Lion Gate." Eliza counted six police officers surrounding the inspector, but Archie squeezed her hand.

"Don't be too hard on them. They may be reporting on what they've found."

"Perhaps, although other than the murder weapon and Mr King, I'm not sure what else they were searching for."

"I didn't see the Kings with the other villagers when we walked across the turning circle." Connie glanced back over her shoulder.

"That's a good point. Me neither." Eliza followed Connie's gaze. "It will be interesting to see if they're still here."

Connie's attention was diverted as they approached a smiling Sergeant Cooper.

"Good afternoon, ladies ... and gents, of course."

"Good afternoon, Sergeant."

At the sound of Archie's voice, Inspector Adams turned and extended his hand to him. "Dr Thomson. And Mr Bell. Are you ready to leave?"

"Almost, but could we have a quick word?" Archie ushered the inspector to one side and held out the package. "We'll need to check it against the wound, but I reckon this is your murder weapon."

The inspector unfolded the coverings. "Where did you find it?"

"We were walking in the Pond Garden and found it in one of the borders near the entrance."

Eliza saw the confusion on the inspector's face. "The Pond Garden's at the opposite side of the palace to the maze." She pointed towards the south-facing wing. "We found it about half an hour ago, but you weren't here, and so we took the liberty of going to the Great Kitchen to ask if it was one of theirs."

"And is it?"

Eliza nodded. "A man dressed in a chef's outfit said he'd

been looking for it this morning, but none of the staff had seen anyone who might have taken it."

"Interesting." Inspector Adams rewrapped the knife. "Thank you all. I'll go along to the kitchens now to see if they'll tell me any more."

"Has anyone identified the body yet?" Mr Bell asked.

"No, if he lived around these parts, he wasn't known to the police. Not any of this lot, anyway." The inspector indicated towards the officers behind him. "I'll call into the local station on Monday and ask if anyone's been reported missing. That's our best option for now."

"The problem is, we don't even know if he was local. He could have come here from London." Eliza faced Mr Bell. "Could you give us any clue as to when you might have met him? Would it have been around here?"

"I wish I knew.' He puffed out his cheeks. "At a guess, I'd say I must have met him years ago. I'm usually quite good with names and faces, and so if I'd met him in London, I expect I'd still remember him."

"Well, it's a start." Inspector Adams made a note. "Did you used to work in Molesey?"

"No, but I worked in Over Moreton about thirty years ago." Mr Bell chuckled to himself. "If that was when I met him, I'm not surprised I can't remember who he is."

Inspector Adams laughed. "I know I wouldn't remember that long ago, especially as he'd look quite different nowadays. You'd better leave it with me. I'll send telegrams to some of the local stations and see what comes back. If I get anything of interest, where's the best place to find you?"

Eliza beamed. "Father's staying with us in Moreton for a couple of weeks. If you get any names, you could bring them over on Monday. If you're early enough, you can join us for luncheon."

"That would be very nice, although I don't suppose I'll have anything by then." He raised his hat. "I'll see you on Monday."

The main entrance of the palace was bathed in sunlight as they headed back to the charabanc. Eliza paused to admire the glistening on the oriel window but was distracted by Mr Hewitt waving at them. "We'd better be going; Mr Hewitt's getting impatient."

"What about Sergeant Cooper? We can't go without him." Connie's voice squeaked as she gazed over to the police officers. "Let me tell him it's time to leave."

Once she was out of earshot, Eliza turned to Archie. "You and Father go and tell Mr Hewitt we won't be a minute. I'll wait for Connie. I doubt Sergeant Cooper will be leaving with us."

"I'd say you're right." Archie indicated towards Connie as she rejoined them.

"He can't leave yet." Her shoulders sagged. "He said he'll catch the train later."

Eliza linked an arm through her friend's. "It's a good job we're here then. Come along, Mr Hewitt's waiting, and I'm sure you'll see the sergeant tomorrow."

The first charabanc had pulled away by the time Archie took the final seat in the second. Eliza rearranged her skirt to give him more room, and they had barely made themselves comfortable when the horses pulled away.

"Oh, I'm so glad we waited for you." Mrs Petty sat to Eliza's left. "I thought you'd have wanted to stay with the police."

"They're nearly finished for the day, so there was no point waiting."

"Did they find out who the dead man was?"

"No, I'm afraid not."

"What about the killer?" Mrs Pitt leaned forward from her seat beside Mrs Petty. "Have they caught him yet?"

"No, we have nothing on him either."

"But we can't have a murderer on the loose so close to Morcton."

Eliza took a deep breath. "I'm afraid these things take time, Mrs Pitt. Inspector Adams will do all he can."

"But you know how to catch murderers…"

Eliza forced herself to smile. "Mrs Pitt, please. It's been a difficult day. Would you mind if I take some time to think things through?"

Mrs Pitt tightened her shoulders and sat back in her seat. "I only asked."

"How are you feeling?" Archie rested his hands on his knees as he faced Mrs Dixon.

"I can't deny I've felt better." Mrs Dixon wafted herself with the fan she held in her hand. "I'll be glad to get away from here, although whether I'll sleep tonight is another matter."

"Don't you worry yourself. I'll write to the doctor in Over Moreton as soon as I get back to the surgery and ask him to call on Monday. If you need a sedative in the meantime, just ask."

"She's staying with me tonight." Mrs Petty smiled at her friend. "We thought it was for the best."

Archie sat back in his seat. "In that case, I'll bring something over for you later."

The bells were ringing for half past four as they pulled up outside the church in Moreton. Mr Hewitt waited at the bottom of the steps as they disembarked.

"Apologies that we're later than planned, but I hope you all had a pleasant day."

"We did, thank you, Mr Hewitt." Mrs Pitt gave Eliza a cursory glance as she linked arms with her husband and marched off.

"And I did too, once I'd got over the shock of finding a dead body." Mrs Petty smirked at Eliza. "It proved to be rather entertaining in the end." She took her friend's arm, failing to spot the alarm on Mrs Dixon's face. "We'd better be going; we'll see you all at church tomorrow."

With the first charabanc empty, the vicar joined them. "I really can't comprehend what she found so interesting."

"It's something out of the ordinary, that's all it is." Eliza lowered her voice and leaned towards Mr Hewitt. "May I ask a question? Were the King family on the charabanc with you?"

Mr Hewitt stiffened. "No. We waited for them as long as possible, but once you were on board, we couldn't waste any more time. These London types take people like me for granted."

"They may have had their reasons."

"Well, I hope they come to church in the morning and apologise. They've not been here five minutes…"

"Don't upset yourself, Mr Hewitt. The rest of us are very grateful for all you do."

"Yes, well, I enjoy doing it, if people appreciate the effort that goes into arranging things."

"I'm sure they do." Eliza glanced across the village green

as Mrs Petty disappeared from view. "I hope Mrs Dixon doesn't have nightmares."

Mr Hewitt followed her gaze. "Poor dear. I'd suggest she gets herself back there, that will be the best way to get over the ordeal."

Connie smiled. "Had you been to Hampton Court before?"

Mr Hewitt straightened his back, his sense of importance restored. "Oh yes, I've been several times. The vicar and I visited about a month ago, as it happens, to check it was a suitable place to visit."

"How lovely. I think we'll go again, now we know how close it is. I'd no idea. We didn't see half of what we'd hoped to."

Mr Hewitt gave a sympathetic smile. "You could spend several days in there."

"At least we found a shortcut on the way back from the maze." Eliza cocked her head to one side. "Did you know you could get to the gardens without going through the palace?"

Mr Hewitt paused. "I did, but I always think the gateway to the path is more like a workman's entrance. I find it's nicer to go through the palace and get a first impression of the Fountain Garden. It's magnificent, don't you think?"

"Yes, I do, and you're right about seeing it immediately from the back of the palace, even if it does take a bit longer to walk that way round. It certainly puts our village green to shame."

Archie rolled his eyes. "Our green is perfectly good enough, now come along. Thank you, Mr Hewitt."

Eliza linked Archie's arm as they bade farewell to the

vicar and walked back to the surgery with Connie and Mr Bell.

Eliza stopped as they reached the gate. "You're very welcome to join us for dinner, Connie."

Connie shuffled her feet. "You're tired; you said so..."

"Only so I didn't have to go into details about the murder with Mrs Pitt. Come on, I insist. With Sergeant Cooper being stuck at the palace, you need cheering up."

The maid met them in the hallway as they walked in. "Would you like a pot of tea, madam?"

"Oh, yes please." Eliza hung her coat on the rack.

"Not for me." Archie walked in the direction of the surgery. "I need to get Mrs Dixon some sleeping draught first. I'll join you later."

Eliza led the way to the living room, where Henry stood by the window, staring at the river as it flowed along the bottom of the garden. He turned around as soon as they entered.

"Finally! I thought you'd be back earlier."

Eliza flopped onto one of the settees, indicating for Connie to join her. "And so we would have, but the day wasn't quite as we expected."

"Why, because the palace was bigger than you imagined?"

"There was that. We'll have to go again to see it all, but no. In fact, you might have wished you'd come with us."

Henry laughed. "Why, did you find a dead body in the maze?"

Eliza sat up straight. "How did you know?"

Henry's eyes flicked between his mother and Connie before he faced Mr Bell. "There wasn't, was there?"

Mr Bell nodded. "I'm afraid so. A chap I'm sure I recognise, but I can't think, for the life of me, who he is."

"Just lying there ... dead?" Henry sat on the settee opposite his mother. "You're fooling me."

"No, we're not."

He slapped a hand on his thigh. "How do I always miss these things? How did he die?"

"We think he was stabbed in the back with a knife from the Great Kitchen."

"You only think? Don't you have any witnesses?"

"Not to the actual murder ... or at least, not so far as they've admitted." Eliza waited while the maid brought in a tray with a pot of tea and four cups and saucers. She set it on the table between the settees and left the room. "We've spoken to three witnesses, who all reported seeing a tall man with dark, greying hair and a beard near the maze at the time. We're assuming that either he saw something that could help us, or that he was the killer."

Henry let out a low whistle. "Did you manage to talk to him?"

"No, he vanished into thin air; but there's a twist. There's a chance the man in question was Mr King from over the road. He matches the description, but we'd better not jump to any conclusions. We need to speak to him and see what he has to say for himself."

"Mr King?" Henry's forehead creased. "What time did you find the body?"

"Around a quarter to eleven, but your father reckons the man hadn't been dead long."

Henry reached for a biscuit. "I'm not sure if this helps, but

Mr King was back in the village by one o'clock. I saw him on my way to The Golden Eagle..."

Eliza sat bolt upright. "You did what? Are you sure?"

"Yes, he was in a carriage with his wife and children. They didn't hang around outside though; as soon as the driver opened the door, he hurried them into the house."

"I bet he did." Without explanation, Eliza dashed to the dining room at the front of the house. *Confound it.*

"What are you doing?"

She jumped at the sound of Henry's voice.

"I wanted to check if the Kings were in, but you can't see the house properly from here."

"Judging by the way he rushed indoors earlier, I don't imagine he'll be putting in an appearance this evening."

Eliza shook her head. "I don't like this; we need to talk to him. Even if it turns out he is innocent, he may have seen something."

Archie had returned from the surgery by the time Eliza scurried back into the living room. "What on earth are you doing?"

"The Kings' were back in the village by one o'clock; don't you think that's suspicious? We've got to go over there and find out what Mr King knows about the murder."

"Wait a minute. You can't go over there by yourself asking questions; you need to tell Inspector Adams, or Sergeant Cooper at the very least, and let them deal with it."

"But they're not here, and we have to do something in case Mr King disappears."

"We've no evidence he'll disappear..."

"But he might ... wouldn't you if you'd just murdered someone and then sneaked away from a church day out?"

Archie groaned. "We don't know any of that's true; there could be a perfectly innocent explanation. His wife may have been ill and wanted to come home, or…"

Eliza gasped. "That's it! If you come with us, we have a legitimate reason to call and check she's all right. They might not want to trouble you on a Saturday evening, but if you visit them…"

"I'm doing no such thing."

"But I can." Henry grinned at his mother. "I'm a qualified doctor now. We can tell them I'm working in the practice over the summer until I move to London. They'll be none the wiser."

Archie struggled to speak. "Don't go encouraging her!"

"But he's absolutely right. We can pay a visit and show our concern as good neighbours and offer Henry's services should anything be wrong." She clapped her hands together. "Splendid."

With the day still bright, Eliza, Connie and Henry walked across the village green to a house in a cul-de-sac opposite.

"Let me do the talking," Eliza said as Henry opened the garden gate for them.

He rolled his eyes at her. "As if we'd do anything else."

A maid answered the door, and at Eliza's request to speak with Mr and Mrs King, she ushered them into an immaculately decorated living room.

"They're about to have dinner, so they'll have no more than five minutes to spare."

"That's fine. We needn't be long."

As soon as the door was closed, Connie wandered to the window. "Goodness, look at these curtains, not to mention the wallpaper. They must have cost a fortune."

"It's these ornaments that are more impressive, the Kings must be real collectors." Eliza picked up one of a pair of solid silver candlesticks.

Henry watched as Eliza placed it back on the sideboard. "I think I've gone into the wrong profession. Why didn't you tell me to be a bank manager, instead of a doctor?"

Eliza raised an eyebrow at him. "You'll do well enough; being a doctor is much more respectable than it once was." She was about to pick up a bowl when the door opened and Mr and Mrs King joined them. Eliza shuddered at the scowl on Mr King's face as he spoke to Henry.

"Mr Thomson, I presume; what can I do for you?"

Eliza forced a smile as she stepped forward to interrupt. "Actually, it was me who asked to speak to you. I noticed you weren't on the charabanc when we left the palace and called to check you're all right."

A frown creased Mr King's forehead. "Why should that be any concern of yours?"

"Forgive me; I'd forgotten that you've only recently moved from London, but it's the way village life works in Moreton. We like to keep an eye on each other, and being the doctor's wife ... and now the mother of a doctor..." she indicated towards Henry "...I tend to make it my business to check that everyone's well."

"I'm sure we're grateful for your concern, but we're fine. Now, if you'll excuse us..."

"Oh, that's a relief; I'll tell Mr Hewitt. He was worried when you didn't travel back with us. Nobody knew you'd left early."

"I wasn't aware we had to check our every movement with Mr Hewitt." Mr King's voice was raised. "If you must know, my wife had a slight headache, and we decided it was best to leave."

"So you *were* feeling under the weather. Are you all right now?"

Before Mrs King could reply, her husband spoke for her. "Yes, she's fine. Now if that's all…"

"Actually, there is one more thing. May I ask what time you left? There was a police barricade across the main entrance from approximately half past eleven, but nobody saw you trying to leave. That was another reason we were worried."

"The police were there?" Mr King stared at Henry, his mouth open, as Eliza continued.

"Yes, unfortunately, there was an incident in the maze at around half past ten. A man was murdered…"

"Enough of that." Mr King put an arm around his wife and escorted her to a seat. "Mrs King has a weak constitution. I'll have no more talk of this."

"I'm sorry, but we need to know when you left the grounds and whether you went near the maze."

"The only time we were close to the maze was when we walked past to get to the Lion Gate. We didn't go to the main entrance. Now, if you don't mind, I really must ask you to leave."

## CHAPTER EIGHT

From behind the counter in her dispensary, Eliza looked out across the village green. *What's Mr King up to?* None of the family had been in church yesterday morning, which hadn't surprised her, but there was something about his manner that didn't sit right. Why would he leave the palace through the Lion Gate, especially when the railway station from Hampton Court was minutes away from the main entrance?

Archie walked into the dispensary with a sheet of paper in his hand. "You're not still dwelling on the Kings, are you? We had enough of that yesterday."

"What do you expect when we don't know what he was up to?"

"I've told you, you can't do any more until Inspector Adams gets here. Is he still joining us for luncheon?"

"I think so, but I haven't heard from him."

"Ah, well, you can make up this prescription while you're waiting." He handed her the paper. "It may help take your mind off things."

Eliza studied it. "Oh good; nothing strenuous." She collected a clean jar from the shelf but spun round when the surgery door opened.

"I hoped I might find you in here." Inspector Adams extended his hand to Archie before raising his hat to Eliza.

"Inspector!" Eliza set down her bottle and moved in front of the counter. "You're earlier than I expected. Have you any news for us?"

"Nothing of note. Once you left the palace on Saturday, I walked to the kitchen to ask about the knife, but got no more from the staff than you did. After that, we removed the barriers and took ourselves home. What about you?"

"Well..." Eliza grinned. "...you may have noticed that Henry wasn't with us for our day out. I was disappointed at first, but it turned out to be rather fortunate. I was telling him about the possibility of Mr King being a suspect, and he said he'd seen the King family come back to the village at around one o'clock."

"Did he now?" The inspector's face brightened. "Maybe I should pay Mr King a visit."

"That may be helpful, he wasn't very talkative to us."

The inspector raised his eyebrows. "You've already spoken to him?"

Eliza kept her face straight. "Mr Hewitt was concerned about him and we wanted to check..."

Archie scowled. "Don't blame Mr Hewitt. You wanted to know what Mr King was up to." He looked over to the inspector. "And believe me, I had nothing to do with it."

"I was only being neighbourly. One of them may have been ill..."

"But assuming they weren't, Mrs Thomson, what did you find out?" The inspector's eyes narrowed.

"Well, he wasn't at all pleased to see us and claimed no knowledge of the murder when we finally mentioned it. Apparently, he left through the Lion Gate because his wife had a headache."

Inspector Adams flicked back through the pages of his notepad. "Weren't we told he was in the Fountain Garden?"

"We were, which made me wonder why he hadn't used the main entrance, but he refused to say anything and asked us to leave."

"Hmm. Perhaps I'll be able to get a little more out of him. In the meantime, the main reason I called is because the local stations have had a few reports of men going missing since Saturday."

"Really, so quickly?"

"It seems to be a common thing on a Monday morning when men don't turn up for work. Employers don't like it."

"I bet they don't." Archie glanced at Eliza.

"Don't look at me like that. If I'm not going to be working, I always tell you."

"Hmm. *Tell* being the operative word."

Eliza tutted. "Take no notice of him, Inspector, he doesn't mean it.

Inspector Adams tried to suppress a smile as his eyes flicked between the two of them. "Maybe I should talk to Mr Bell instead. I've a few names to show him. Is he at home?"

Eliza grinned. "He is. Let me show you through to the living room. He should have finished the crossword by now."

Mr Bell was dozing in a chair by the window when Eliza opened the door. "We've a visitor, Father."

Mr Bell immediately sat up straight. "Inspector Adams, it's good to see you again."

"And you, Mr Bell." The inspector offered him his hand before pulling a sheet of paper from his pocket. "I've a list of men who've been reported missing by their employers this morning. I'm hoping it might jog your memory with regards to our victim."

Mr Bell took the paper. "My, there are more here than I'd imagined." He pondered the list then tapped his index finger alongside one entry. "I think this could be our man. Mr Gerard Hobson. I recall him now; he started work at Royal's not long before I left. A machinist if I remember rightly; my, that takes me back."

Inspector Adams made a note of the name. "He was reported missing from Molesey. Are you certain it was him?"

"I'm as sure as I can be, thirty years after the event. He could have moved on from Royal's."

"Very well, we'll need to confirm it, but at least we've something to work with. The next question is, 'Why would anyone want to kill him?' Do you remember anything of relevance?"

Mr Bell sighed. "Not really. He'd already completed his apprenticeship when he joined Royal's, so I guess he was in his early twenties when I met him. I seem to think he was a troubled chap, but old Mr Royal took him under his wing."

"Can you give us any more information about the cause of his worries?"

"No, I'm afraid I can't. We didn't work together directly, and as I say, I left not long after he started."

"Very well. I'd better get Sergeant Cooper over there this afternoon to find out what happened to him." He turned to

Eliza. "Would it be an inconvenience if I missed luncheon? I really should be getting back to the station."

Eliza shook her head. "Not at all; we can postpone it until after the killer's behind bars, although ... would you mind if Mrs Appleton and I go with Sergeant Cooper?"

Archie scowled. "Why on earth do you need to go?"

"Don't say it like that. The sergeant appreciates our help. Please, Inspector. Just to be sure he asks the right questions. We've helped him before..."

The inspector nodded. "Very well, as long as it's clear Sergeant Cooper is in charge."

"Naturally! Shall we meet him at the police station at one o'clock?"

Sergeant Cooper was waiting outside the station door when they arrived, and he flashed Connie a broad smile.

"Good afternoon, Mrs Appleton. And you too, Mrs Thomson. I must say this is a lovely surprise. Inspector Adams has just told me you'll be travelling with me."

Connie lowered her eyes as the sergeant gazed at her. "Good afternoon, Sergeant. I hope you don't mind us joining you."

"Now, don't you be silly, Mrs Appleton. You know it's always a pleasure. Shall we?" He indicated the carriage standing on the opposite side of the road. "I must admit, I expected him to come himself."

Eliza made herself comfortable. "I thought the same thing, but I got the feeling he had something else on this afternoon."

"Well, whatever the reason, I'd prefer you two ladies for company." He took his seat opposite Connie and motioned to the driver to move off. "So, from what the inspector told me, we're asking about a Mr Hobson who used to work at Royal's. Do you know anything about him?"

"Not really. It's to be hoped Father remembered him correctly. We'll look rather foolish if he's identified the wrong man."

Connie giggled. "Maybe that's why the inspector didn't want to come with us."

Eliza groaned. "Can you imagine? I only hope this isn't a wasted visit."

The ride to Over Moreton took little more than five minutes, and Eliza inspected the single-storey red-brick building as they came to a stop outside Royal & Sons' workshop. "I always wondered why the brickwork of these buildings was so dirty until we went inside and saw what they did. I've no idea how they work with that big furnace in this weather."

Sergeant Cooper jumped down from the carriage and reached back to help each lady alight. "It's hard work for sure. Hopefully, we'll be in and out quickly enough."

The workshop was much the same as the last time Eliza and Connie had visited, with a multitude of men making a tremendous noise around a large furnace to one side of the room. Thankfully, young Mr Royal was in the workshop, and Sergeant Cooper arranged to talk in his office.

"Good afternoon, ladies." Mr Royal offered them both a seat while Sergeant Cooper stood behind them. Eliza thought Mr Royal had aged in the two years since they'd last visited; his brown hair was showing signs of grey, and a wrinkle or two stayed in position around his eyes when his smile dropped. Not that she was surprised, given he worked in conditions like this.

"So what can I do for you? As far as I'm aware, we've no employees who are missing at the moment."

Eliza cast her mind back to the last time they'd called, while Sergeant Cooper asked about Mr Hobson. The creases on Mr Royal's forehead deepened as they spoke.

"A Mr Hobson? The name rings a bell, but if he worked here thirty years ago, it must have been around the time I started my apprenticeship. I should remember him if he was here for any length of time." He wandered over to a large wooden cabinet. "My father was never one for throwing things away, so there could be something in here."

He drew out a wad of papers and placed them on his desk, where he flicked through them. "Now, what's this? It looks like he didn't stay long, five years at the most. That would explain why I don't remember him. I am usually good with ex-employees."

"Would you have any idea why he left?"

Mr Royal turned over the sheet of paper and continued reading. "Hmm. He must have got himself into a bit of trouble because he was dismissed, but it doesn't give any details." He flicked through several more sheets of papers. "No, there's nothing else. It's funny I've no memory of him, though. If he was sacked, I'd expect quite a to-do, but I don't recall anything."

Eliza raised an eyebrow. "That's interesting. Do the records mention where he moved to?"

"No, not that I can see, although it says here, he was originally from Molesey. He may have gone back."

"We'll be able to find out easily enough." Sergeant Cooper's voice quietened Eliza. "It's not a big place, and it has its own police station. If he's ever been in trouble over there, they should know ... if they've kept their records."

Mr Royal stood up to show them out. "I hope you find what you're looking for. If I remember anything else, I'll send over an errand boy to tell you."

## CHAPTER NINE

Eliza stepped out of the workshop and scanned the expanse of gravel to the front. The only area offering any shade was beneath the branches of a large oak tree that stood adjacent to the road, in the front corner of the plot. She wasted no time in pointing it out to Connie.

"I don't know how they work in there. The office wasn't even close to the furnace, and it was still hot."

Connie took a fan from her handbag. "Thank goodness I put this in." She moved next to Eliza and fanned the two of them.

"That's better." Eliza lifted her chin as the cool air flicked over her. "What is it about that man that makes everyone forget who he is?"

"Maybe it's because he didn't stay anywhere for long." Sergeant Cooper gestured towards the carriage. "Shall we go?"

Eliza paused to study the building. "Mr Royal may be in charge here, but he's not the oldest. I'd hazard a guess that there are men here who'd remember Mr Hobson."

The sergeant followed her gaze. "Would you like to go back in?"

"No. I don't want to appear impolite to Mr Royal, and he may not like us disturbing his workers." Eliza stared at the sergeant. "I imagine they'll take a break during the afternoon. It may be better to have an informal chat. Do you think they'd come outside for some air?"

"On a day like today it wouldn't surprise me, but we could have rather a long wait. I doubt they'll come outside until three o'clock, which is still an hour off."

"Hmm. Are you in a hurry?"

"I'd better tell the inspector that a trip to Molesey is in order, and I told Constable Jenkins I'd be back for brew time."

"Would you mind if we stay here and wait while you do that? We could take a walk around the village to pass the time. I've not been here for months."

Sergeant Cooper glanced at Connie. "Very well, you do that and I'll come back and pick you up at four o'clock. How does that sound?"

Eliza's face broke into a broad smile. "Splendid. Thank you."

Connie gave the sergeant a coy wave as the carriage pulled away from the workshop. Eliza grinned at her.

"It's rather handy having the two of you walking out together. He's very eager to please."

"He was always helpful."

"He was, but he wouldn't have offered to come and collect us before."

Connie flushed. "I'm sure he would; anyway, where do

you want to walk? I doubt it will take us an hour to cover the whole of Over Moreton."

"No, it won't, but we can walk up the high street to see what's happening and return here in good time for three o'clock. I'd hate to miss anyone."

The stroll turned out to be shorter and more uneventful than Eliza had hoped, and by quarter to three they were once again standing outside the workshop.

"It could be a long wait until four o'clock if nobody steps outside." Eliza huffed as they retook their spot under the tree. "They really need a bench here too. And some more shade."

Connie laughed. "I don't suppose they have many ladies waiting at the side of the road."

Eliza studied the front of the workshop. "The men would probably like to sit down, too, given they're on their feet all day. Perhaps they'd appreciate a verandah; they've enough room."

Connie indicated towards the building. "Why don't we ask them? There are two over there now."

Eliza chuckled. "Not now, we've more important things to talk about. Come along, let's see what they've got to say."

The men stood by the door to the workshop and removed their caps to wipe the sweat from their balding heads.

"Hopefully, they'll be old enough to remember." Eliza strode over to them while Connie stayed a step behind.

"Good afternoon, gentlemen. May we have a word with you?"

A man with an impressively bushy moustache, who appeared to be the older of the two, eyed them suspiciously. "You were with that police officer."

"Yes, that's right. We were hoping to find out about a Mr

Hobson who used to work here. We wondered if you remembered him."

"If Mr Royal hasn't told you anything, then we've nothing to add."

"Oh, you misunderstand." Eliza flashed them a smile. "Mr Royal was very helpful, but he's too young to remember the man himself. We hoped you might know more of the details, assuming you worked here at the time."

The younger man's eyes narrowed. "What did Mr Royal tell you?"

"Only what he found in some old notes. The records showed Mr Hobson was here for about five years but he left, possibly because he was sacked. Might you remember why that was?"

The men exchanged glances before the older one spoke. "He was a strange chap; never really took to anyone except old Mr Royal. I can't imagine why he'd get rid of him."

"There was all that money that disappeared." The younger man scratched his head as he stared at his colleague.

"I'd clean forgotten about that."

Eliza's eyes flicked between the pair of them. "What money would that be?"

"I don't know exact details, but I remember around about that time small amounts of money started disappearing from the office. Every few weeks or so, it was."

"That's right." The lines on the older man's forehead faded. "There were rumours that Mr Hobson was the one with light fingers, but old Mr Royal wouldn't entertain any talk of larceny."

"But eventually he sacked him?" Eliza raised an eyebrow.

"I'm not sure about that." The younger man's speech was

slow. "All I know is that one morning Mr Royal came into the workshop and told us a large amount of money had gone missing. He seemed unusually troubled by it."

"And was Mr Hobson the main suspect?"

"He was, but as usual, Mr Royal refused to press charges." The man shook his head. "I don't know why he was so loyal to him, but about a week later he left."

The older man nodded. "We were never told he'd been sacked, though."

"How strange." Connie's brow creased. "Did the thefts end once he'd gone?"

The younger man gazed into the distance. "Now you mention it, they did, although we didn't think much about it at the time. Probably because we all assumed he was guilty."

"And did you see him again?"

Both men shook their heads, and Eliza continued.

"The thing is, Mr Hobson was found murdered in the maze at Hampton Court Palace last Saturday, and we need to find out if anyone had reason to want him dead."

The younger man blew out through his lips. "Murdered? Well, if he carried on like he did here, there could be any number with a grudge."

"But you've not seen him for what, twenty-five years?

The older man shrugged. "Something like that. I think he moved up to London when he left here, but whereabouts, I couldn't say. Someone who might know is his brother. He often mentioned him, not in complimentary terms, mind you, but he may have an address for him. He was over in Molesey somewhere, but whether he's still there, I've no idea."

Eliza gave them a genuine smile. "Thank you, that's very helpful. You don't happen to have the brother's Christian name, do you? The dead man was Mr Gerard Hobson. We need to be clear who we're looking for."

Both men once again shook their heads as the older man spoke.

"I'm afraid I've no idea. He may have mentioned it, but the old memory..."

Eliza brandished her notebook. "That's why I write everything down."

For the first time, the man smiled. "I don't blame you. Now, if that's everything, we'd better get back to work."

"There's one more thing. Does anyone else work here who may remember him? Or perhaps kept in touch with him after he left?"

He screwed up his face. "I doubt it, but let me ask around. If there is, I'll send them out."

"Thank you. That's most kind."

With no further visitors, the remaining half an hour dragged, and Eliza gave an audible sigh as the police carriage pulled into view.

"Bless Sergeant Cooper for being early, my feet are in agony." She skipped from one foot to the other as the horses slowed to a halt. "I'll need to make a rub to go on them tonight."

"You can make some for me, too, if you don't mind." Connie smiled at the sergeant as he climbed down to meet them.

"Good afternoon, ladies. Have you had an enjoyable few hours?"

"We've had some success, but may we tell you about it once we sit down?" Eliza put a foot on the bottom step of the carriage. "Shoes with heels are not meant to be stood up in for too long."

Connie giggled. "Don't look so shocked, Sergeant. We're only talking about our feet."

"Well, yes." His cheeks reddened. "Let me help you inside."

Thankful she had no one sitting opposite her, Eliza stretched out her legs to relieve the throbbing in her feet. "Ooh, that's better." She waited for Sergeant Cooper to take his seat. "You'll be pleased to hear we've got some information for you."

"Really?" The sergeant pulled out his notepad as the carriage moved off. "You really are a marvel, Mrs Thomson; and you too, Mrs Appleton."

"We might not have learned as much as we'd like, but we spoke to two gentlemen who remembered Mr Hobson. It seems he was regularly accused of stealing from the business, but old Mr Royal never pressed charges. It was only after the last, most significant theft, that he finally left."

"And there were no charges for that either?"

"Apparently not."

"The thefts ended once he'd left, and so everyone assumed he was the thief," Connie added.

"That's good to know." Sergeant Cooper's eyes sparkled as he smiled at Connie; Eliza pretended not to notice.

"The other piece of interesting information is that Mr Hobson had a brother. He lived in Molesey at the time, and they suggested he may be a good place to start if we want to know where the murdered man went to once he left Over Moreton."

Sergeant Cooper returned to his notepad. "A brother?

Well then, let's hope he stayed in Molesey. Perhaps our victim moved in with him."

Eliza shook her head. "They didn't think so, they thought he'd gone off to London…"

Sergeant Cooper groaned. "That won't make things easy. He could be anywhere."

"That's my concern. Have you any idea when we'll be going to Molesey?"

The sergeant stuttered. "Erm, well, I couldn't say … it will be up to the inspector. I imagine he'll want to go."

Eliza nodded. "I suppose he will. Would you tell him we're free tomorrow afternoon? We should strike while the iron's hot."

## CHAPTER TEN

The morning was drawing to a close as Eliza put away the last of her jars and lined up the prescriptions under the counter, ready for either collection or delivery. Not that she was paying much attention to what she was doing. *I should have heard from Inspector Adams by now if we're travelling to Molesey. It would be nice to be given a bit of warning.*

The maid was about to hit the gong for luncheon when Eliza reached the dining room door.

"That was good timing. Has Dr Thomson come through?"

"No, not yet, madam. Let me ring this so he knows the time."

Eliza stood with her hands over her ears while the maid gave the gong a single strike. The noise echoed around the hall, but the maid didn't wait for it to subside as she hung up the rubber hammer and turned to go back to the kitchen.

"One moment, did Inspector Adams or Sergeant Cooper call this morning?"

The maid shook her head. "We've had no visitors this

morning, except the postman, of course. Shall I fetch the mail while you wait for Dr Thomson?"

Eliza spotted Henry and Mr Bell emerge from the living room. "No, thank you. It will keep."

Eliza waited for them to sit down. "Have either of you seen Inspector Adams today?"

"I saw the police carriage leave the village this morning," Henry said. "It must have been about ten o'clock when I was on my way to the shop."

Eliza bit on her lip.

"What's the matter?" Archie joined them and took his seat just as the maid placed four plates on the table.

"I told Inspector Adams we needed to visit Molesey to see if they could find Mr Hobson's brother. I assumed Connie and I would go with him, but by the sounds of it, they've gone without us."

"You don't know that." Mr Bell picked up his knife and fork. "They could have been going anywhere."

Eliza sighed. "I suppose so, but I'll walk up there later with Connie and find out what they're up to."

Constable Jenkins was manning the desk when Eliza and Connie arrived at the station.

"Good afternoon, ladies." He grinned at Connie. "Are you here for Sergeant Cooper?"

"Good afternoon, Constable." Eliza placed both hands on the counter. "We've actually come to see Inspector Adams. Is he here?"

"No, sorry, Mrs Thomson. He and the sergeant disappeared off to Molesey this morning, and I've not seen them since."

Eliza took a deep breath. "I don't suppose they said when they'd be back?"

"I'm afraid not. They weren't entirely sure what they were looking for, so they could be a while. Shall I tell them you called?"

Eliza studied the constable. "Yes, why don't you. They can call at the surgery if they need me."

Constable Jenkins held open the door as they stepped back outside and Eliza glanced over her shoulder to check he'd closed it again.

"I told you that's where they'd gone. Why didn't they take us with them? They know we can help."

"Maybe something came up and they needed to leave in a hurry."

"I doubt it. They probably think they'll solve this on their own, but they wouldn't even know about Molesey if it wasn't for us." Eliza gazed across the village green. "We'll see how far they get."

"What shall we do now? Do you want to sit on a bench?"

"No. I'd rather not be here when they come back. I'll tell you what, why don't we visit Mrs Petty? We've not seen much of her since the outing, and we could do with asking after Mrs Dixon."

"Yes, that would be nice, and she's always pleased to see us."

The walk to their neighbour's house was short, and Mrs Petty saw them from her living room window. She was at the front door before they'd walked up the garden path.

"Good afternoon, Mrs Petty."

"Good afternoon, ladies. How lovely to see you." Mrs

Petty held open the door and ushered them inside, offering them a seat in the window.

"How are you keeping?" Eliza smoothed her skirt as she took her seat. "We called to ask after you and Mrs Dixon. Have you both recovered from your ordeal?"

"Oh, we're fine now." Mrs Petty straightened the cushions on the empty chairs. "Mrs Dixon went home yesterday quite her usual self."

"That's a relief. It was a nasty shock for the two of you."

"It was indeed, but we're made of stern stuff. Have you heard how the investigation's coming along?" Mrs Petty's eyes twinkled. "I saw you wandering up to the police station."

Eliza chuckled. "Not much gets past you. Unfortunately, the inspector and Sergeant Cooper were out, so we're not sure if there's any more news."

"Haven't you found out anything yourself? You don't usually wait to be told."

Eliza laughed. "You're right, I don't. In fact, we worked out yesterday who the murdered man was. His name was Mr Gerard Hobson and we believe he lived in Molesey. We don't have any details of where he was working, but Father recognised him from the time he spent at Royal's in Over Moreton."

"My, that must have been some years ago."

"Thirty, to be precise. It's strange though, because although he was there for about five years, very few people remember him."

Mrs Petty paused. "Hmm. Mr Hobson. I've a feeling I've come across the name before, but then I suppose it's quite common."

"The thing is, he was sacked from Royal's when they

suspected him of stealing a large amount of money. For some reason, old Mr Royal wouldn't press charges, but he left shortly afterwards."

Connie rested her hands on her lap as she leaned forward to speak to Mrs Petty. "Are you all right? You've gone rather quiet."

Mrs Petty stood up. "I am, I'm trying to remember something. Let me go and make a pot of tea; it will help me think."

Connie sat back and gazed out of the window as two young women pushed prams across the green. "It's such a marvellous view of the village from here. The perfect house for Mrs Petty."

"It's just a shame you can't see the Kings' house. I can't shake the feeling he's hiding something."

"Oh, look." Connie leaned forward as a carriage drove past the surgery. "Sergeant Cooper and Inspector Adams. Shall we walk back to the station?"

"And miss out on a cup of tea? I don't think so." Eliza relaxed into her chair. "As I said to Constable Jenkins, they know where we are if they want us."

"Here we are, ladies." Mrs Petty arrived with a large tray full with a teapot, cups, saucers and a delightful Victoria sponge cake.

"Ooh, lovely." Connie helped steady the tray as Mrs Petty put it on the table.

"You came on the right day. I always do a bit of baking on a Tuesday morning." Mrs Petty stirred the tea in the pot before pouring out three cups.

Connie chuckled. "We must remember that. I'm behind with my chores this week, with things being as they are."

With three slices of cake cut, Mrs Petty took her seat. "I've remembered why I know that name. A Mr Hobson was in the newspaper several months ago. I don't remember exactly what the story was about, but I seem to think he stood as a witness in a trial. He gave evidence that would have sent someone to jail."

A smile brightened Eliza's face. "You don't remember when this was, do you?"

"No, that's what's puzzling me. It was definitely this year, probably before Easter, so I'd take a guess at March."

"Do you remember where they held the trial?"

"It was local, so it will have been in Kingston-upon-Thames."

Eliza cocked her head to one side. "So they cover Molesey as well?"

"Oh, certainly. It doesn't take long to get from one place to the other if you drive through the park around the palace."

Eliza took out her notebook. "I really should learn the geography of the area better. I've been back in Moreton for three years now."

"It's to be expected if you've no need to go that way. Mr Petty would regularly take me to the palace when we were first married. It always made a pleasant day out."

"Ah! That's how you got to the centre of the maze so quickly." Eliza grinned. "You'd already been."

Mrs Petty was sheepish. "I hadn't been for many a year. For all I knew it may have changed."

Eliza smirked as she reread her notes. "All right, I believe you, but can I get something straight? If the Mr Hobson you read about in the newspaper is the same Mr Hobson who lived in Molesey, and is also the man you found in the maze, that means he'd recently accused someone of theft ... but they were found not guilty?"

"Precisely."

"So, the next question must be, who was the man accused? If I'd had to stand trial, I'd be furious with Mr Hobson. It gives the accused man a good motive to want him dead, don't you think?"

"Gosh, yes." Connie's forehead creased. "But how do we find that out?"

"Assuming they have a library, we'll have to make a trip to Kingston. They should have copies of the old newspapers." Eliza turned to Mrs Petty.

"Yes, indeed. I've not been myself, but I've been told they have a good archive."

"Splendid." Eliza looked at Connie. "I know what we'll be doing tomorrow."

Mrs Petty pointed out of the window. "As much as I've enjoyed your company, I suspect you may want to hurry home; Inspector Adams has arrived at the surgery."

"Goodness, you're right. We'd better go." Eliza placed her cup and saucer back on the tray. "Thank you for the tea and the information. If we find anything else out, we'll come and let you know."

Mrs Petty led them to the door. "That's good enough for me."

By the time they reached the gate to the surgery, both Eliza and Connie were worn out.

"Thank goodness the green is no bigger." Eliza put a hand to her chest as she paused for breath.

"Quite." Connie smirked. "I'm glad you're the one who does all the talking."

Eliza rolled her eyes. "I'm hoping Inspector Adams will do a good deal of explaining as to why they went off to Molesey without us."

"You'd better go and ask him then."

The maid had obviously seen Eliza arrive home and opened the front door as soon as they approached.

"Inspector Adams is in the living room with Dr Thomson and Mr Bell, madam."

"Thank you, we'll be there in a minute."

With their coats hanging in the hall and their breath recovered, Eliza led Connie into the back room.

"Inspector Adams, here you are. Did Constable Jenkins mention we were looking for you?"

The inspector gave a faint smile. "Mrs Thomson, Mrs Appleton. Apologies we didn't tell you we were going to Molesey, but we had to leave at short notice, and I assumed you'd be working."

Eliza raised an eyebrow. "What was the sudden urgency?"

"We'd had a telegram to say that the police in Molesey were aware of a Mr Hobson and they were waiting for us to visit."

*Which I'm sure could have waited until this afternoon.* "Oh, that's good. So what did you find out?"

"That the victim was indeed the Mr Gerard Hobson who used to work in Over Moreton. For several years, he'd been a foreman at a railway parts company in Molesey. Quite a large workshop near the railway station. The thing is, prior to that, he was a successful businessman in London, which explains why he was always smartly dressed whenever he was outside the workshop."

"That's good to know. Well done, Father." Eliza allowed herself a smile as Mr Bell grinned back at her.

"I'm just pleased my memory's still working."

"You'll be glad to learn that the owner of the business, a Mr Coates, was able to identify the body too. That's why we were back later than expected." Inspector Adams raised himself up onto the balls of his feet.

"Splendid. This is all proceeding nicely." Eliza smiled as she paced the floor. "So, now we know who the victim is, we need to find out who wanted him dead." She glanced at the inspector. "Did you manage to track down the brother while you were in Molesey? He could help."

"I'm afraid not. We asked all the men at the workshop, but none of them knew of a brother. We also checked at the police station and they had no knowledge of another Mr Hobson either."

Eliza studied her father. "Would that be unusual in a village like Molesey?"

"I suppose he could have lived a quiet life and not come to their attention. I don't imagine the police know everyone."

Eliza took a seat on the settee beside Connie. "Perhaps we need to keep searching then."

"Or maybe you don't need to bother." Archie leaned forward in his chair and smirked at the inspector. "Inspector Adams has another name to work on."

Eliza's eyes widened. "Go on."

The inspector cleared his throat. "A number of the men in the factory said that a man called Swift visited the workshop approximately once a month. They never found out why, because he and Mr Hobson would always go outside, but they described him as tall with dark, greying hair and a neatly trimmed beard and moustache."

"The man who was seen at the maze?" Eliza stared at the inspector.

"Exactly."

"Mr Swift." She slumped back in her seat. "So it wasn't Mr King."

"It doesn't look like it. In fact, that was the main reason I called. We need to leave him alone. He's a very influential man and we can't go upsetting him."

Eliza's stomach churned. "I suppose I owe him an apology. Not that he'll welcome me calling again."

"No, I don't suppose he will." Archie scowled at her. "Sometimes you need to know when to leave well alone."

"All right, I promise I won't go near him." She grimaced at Inspector Adams. "Is he really influential?"

"Well, he's the manager of the local bank in Kingston, if that's influential enough."

*Oh no.* Eliza put a hand to her head. "That's all I need."

"Why?"

"No reason, other than we're going to the library in Kingston tomorrow. I hope we don't bump into him."

"Since when did you decide that?" Archie glared across at her. "I won't be able to escort you, and what about the prescriptions?"

"We were going to go after surgery. Mrs Petty remembered that Mr Hobson was a witness in a trial early this year. The accused was found not guilty, but I wondered if the ordeal was enough to give him a motive for murder. Apparently, Kingston library has a good archive of old newspapers, so I want to check whether we can find out more about the people associated with the case to see if it gives us anything else to go on."

"It's worth a try." Inspector Adams seemed suitably impressed. "I don't remember the case myself."

"As worthy as it may be, I'm still not happy about you going alone."

"Don't worry." Eliza sat up straight again. "I'll ask Henry to join us. He's been itching to get involved for a day or two; he'll be delighted."

## CHAPTER ELEVEN

Eliza was used to tidying the dispensary in a hurry, but today she was in a particular rush. The possibility of finding evidence in the newspaper for an investigation she was involved with was more than she could have hoped for. Her years of following crimes for a hobby were about to pay off.

"Henry, are you nearly ready?" She wandered into the living room where her son sat with her father.

Mr Bell glanced up at her. "Are you not waiting to have luncheon?"

"No, Cook has made us some sandwiches to take with us. We can eat them in the carriage on the way there." Eliza beamed. "Don't you think that's exciting?"

Mr Bell shuddered. "It sounds very messy to me. Give me a table and a knife and fork any day."

Eliza laughed. "It's as well you're not joining us then. Are you ready, Henry?"

"I am, and the horse and carriage are waiting outside.

Shall I fetch Mrs Appleton while you get your hat and coat on?"

"If you wouldn't mind. I'll meet you outside."

With a final farewell to Archie, Eliza hurried down the garden path. She was about to follow Henry to Connie's house when Mrs Petty waved to her from the path across the village green.

"Oh, I'm glad I caught you. I remembered a little more about the trial last night and thought it may help. It was a burglary at a workshop in Molesey, where Mr Hobson was a foreman. He accused one of the employees of taking a large amount of money. It caused quite a scandal if I remember rightly, and even though the employee was found innocent, he still lost his job and had to move from his lodgings."

"That would be reason enough to hold a grudge, I should imagine."

"I thought the same. The only thing I'm cross with myself about is that I can't recall the name of the accused man. I racked my brains last night, but it just won't come to me."

Eliza smiled as she saw Connie and Henry approaching. "Well, hopefully, one of us will find something at the library. If we get a name, I'll call and tell you to put you out of your misery."

Once the carriage set off, Eliza unpacked a wicker basket the cook had prepared. "This is almost as exciting as going to the library. Let's see what we've got. Cheese with cream, roast beef with salad, and egg. Shall we all have one of each?"

"We'd better save the lemonade until we stop though." Connie eyed the bottle of cloudy liquid. "It could get messy."

Eliza handed out the plates and offered around the basket.

"We'd better be quick, we need to be finished by the time we get to Kingston."

Henry bit into a cheese sandwich. "Don't worry, the driver will wait. Now, what do you want us to look for this afternoon?"

"Mrs Petty said it was a court case for a burglary that took place earlier this year. She thinks it was in March, although it could be February or early April. She's fairly certain it was before Easter."

"So the burglary was in Molesey?" Henry helped himself to a beef sandwich.

"Yes, probably at the place where Mr Hobson worked. He was a foreman and stood as a witness. Any details will be of interest, but I particularly want to know the name of the accused man, or anyone who may have been with him. Other people who testified against him or those who gave him character references. Anything like that."

"I can manage that, as long as the library has the newspapers." Henry indicated the approaching high street. "I think we're almost there. We'd better get these sandwiches eaten."

The smell of old leather struck Eliza as soon as they walked through the door, and she inhaled a deep breath as she gazed at the rows of books encased in their mahogany shelving. It was like being back at Bedford College all those years ago. The librarian studied them as they made their way across the foyer, clearly uncomfortable with their presence.

"They're with me." Henry edged in front of his mother to stand by the counter. "We'd like to study some of your newspapers from earlier this year. Could you point us in the right direction?"

The man gave Eliza a hard stare before he stepped away and led them to a table at the far end of the room.

"If you'll wait here, I'll have them brought to you." He observed Eliza and Connie. "May I point out that talking isn't allowed in the library?"

Eliza curled down the corners of her lips as he disappeared. "Give these men a bit of responsibility and it goes straight to their heads."

Henry shook his head. "And with good reason. Be quiet!"

They waited in silence until two errand boys appeared and placed armfuls of newspapers on the table in front of Henry.

"If you need anything else, sir, please ask at the desk." The boy spoke in hushed tones.

Eliza counted to three as she watched them disappear. "As long as sir's happy…"

Henry put a hand on hers. "Come on, don't be like that, you know what these places are like, and we have work to do. Where shall we start?"

Eliza flicked through the newspapers. "Henry, you do February while Connie does April. I'll take March."

Henry groaned. "I can't think why. Let's hope Mrs Petty got her dates right."

"Shh! No talking." The librarian paced across the room, glaring at them.

Henry put a hand to his mouth to stifle a laugh. "Sorry."

They spread themselves out along the length of the table and worked methodically, turning each page slowly to digest the headlines. Occasionally there was a false alarm when a court case appeared similar to the one they were searching for, but by two o'clock, Eliza was beginning to think Mrs Petty had made it up. "I'm sure she said it was in the *Surrey Comet*."

"Could it have been earlier than she remembered?" Connie whispered as the librarian once more stared at her.

Eliza sighed. "I suppose so. Henry, will you go and ask for the papers from January?"

They waited a full ten minutes for them to arrive, and Eliza divided the pile between them. Connie was on her second newspaper when she let out a squeal.

"Here."

"Quiet, please!" The librarian strode to the edge of the table. "I won't warn you again."

Connie put a hand over her mouth as she pointed to the article. The librarian seemed unimpressed, but Eliza and Henry closed in on either side of her.

"Well, well, well." Eliza took the notebook from her bag. "Let me write this down."

Fortunately, it wasn't a long article, and five minutes later, with the details copied out, she stood up to leave. "It looks like another trip to Hampton Court Palace is in order."

Connie waited until they were outside before she spoke. "Will we tell Inspector Adams and Sergeant Cooper we're going to the palace? I imagine they'll want to come with us."

Eliza screwed up her nose. "I'd rather not. After what happened with the trip to Molesey, it wouldn't surprise me if they stop us going again."

"But they won't know anything about this if we don't tell them." Henry led the way back to the carriage. "I say we should go."

Eliza chuckled. "He's his mother's son."

"Maybe he is, but we shouldn't go without telling

Sergeant Cooper. Or at least I shouldn't; I don't want him to be angry with me."

Eliza followed Connie into the carriage. "He won't mind. We've done things like this before."

"But this is different. We're walking out together now."

Eliza patted Connie's hand. "Let's finish this lemonade and we can have a think about it. It's already three o'clock. If we drive over to Moreton for permission, there won't be time to travel to the palace, but perhaps we can suggest a visit tomorrow."

With a reluctant nod, Connie accepted a glass. "Very well. I suppose it's different if we all go together."

Eliza was in no hurry to get back to Moreton, and asked the driver if he'd take them via Molesey so they could see the workshop. The road took them through the park along the side of the palace.

"There's the Lion Gate." She gestured towards the ornate iron gates that sat between two impressive stone pillars. "Is that why Mr King left the way he did, because he travelled to Kingston on his way home? I suppose he'd be familiar with the route given he works there."

"It makes sense." Henry peered through the window to catch a glimpse of the grounds beyond the entrance. "I'll have to come with you next time; it looks as if I missed a good day out."

"We could call now, if you like. We'll have time before they close."

"No." Connie grabbed Eliza's hand. "Please don't."

"Very well. Let's have a quick drive around Molesey and then we'll go straight to the police station in Moreton."

Sergeant Cooper was on the desk when they arrived and

gave Connie a broad smile. "You're back. Did you have a nice afternoon out?"

"We did, thank you, and we've called to tell you what we found out." Connie's face was beaming. "You'll never guess..."

Eliza held up a hand. "Perhaps Inspector Adams should be here as well so we don't have to go through everything twice."

Eliza hadn't finished talking when the inspector appeared from the back office.

"Did I hear my name mentioned?"

"You did. I thought we should tell you both together what we learned at the library."

"Splendid. Why don't you all come through and take a seat?" He stood at the door as everyone filed in. "So, it was a worthwhile visit?"

"Yes, indeed. We found the court case Mrs Petty told us about. It took us longer than we hoped because it was held in January. It related to possible larceny in September of the previous year, and apparently it was Mr Hobson who insisted on making the prosecution."

"And the man accused?"

"Now that's where it's interesting. I suspect you didn't meet him when you were at the palace, but we did. It was one of the gardeners. A Mr Turner. Not only that, he was seen in the maze shortly before Mrs Dixon found the body. When we spoke to him, he said he'd only gone over there to pick up his shears."

"He said he didn't know Mr Hobson, didn't he?" Sergeant Cooper's brow creased.

"He did, and another gardener gave him a plausible alibi, which is why we haven't focused on him."

Sergeant Cooper shook his head. "It could all have been set up in advance. You mark my words, he sounds like a bad 'un. Besides, if he used to be in a workshop, what's he doing working as a gardener?"

"It would appear he's not been at the palace long, which makes me wonder if he only took the job because he'd been forced to leave his old one. I suggest we go back and speak to him again tomorrow."

"We're grateful for the information, Mrs Thomson, but we can take it from here." The inspector's voice was firm.

"But..."

"Please, Mrs Thomson. No buts. Sergeant Cooper and I will go over there first thing tomorrow morning and find out why he lied."

"But you can't arrest him, not yet." Eliza held the inspector's gaze. "Please, there's not enough evidence yet, and I imagine he went through enough with the other trial. You will be civil to him?"

Inspector Adams stood up tall. "Let's see what he's got to say for himself. If he cooperates, we'll go easy on him. I can't say fairer than that."

## CHAPTER TWELVE

Try as she might, Eliza couldn't focus the following morning. The prescriptions had been arriving too quickly for her to deal with, and she really didn't want to make small talk with the patients when there was a chance the police could arrest a potentially innocent man.

As midday approached, she was about to leave the dispensary when the door opened and Inspector Adams walked in.

"Inspector!"

"Mrs Thomson. Have I called at a good time?"

Eliza walked around the counter towards him. "Yes, I was about to go through for luncheon. Will you join us?"

He shook his head. "Thank you, but I'd better not. I only wanted to update you on what we learned this morning."

"Did you speak to Mr Turner?"

"We did, and I must admit I'm glad I accompanied Sergeant Cooper. We may have had a man in custody if I hadn't."

Eliza put a hand to her chest. "That's a relief. Don't you think he was involved with the murder?"

"I wouldn't go so far as to say that, but as you said, there isn't enough evidence to charge him at the moment."

Eliza's eyes narrowed. "Did he confess to knowing Mr Hobson?"

The inspector grimaced. "Only once I told him we were aware of the trial. He said he realised it looked suspicious, which is why he hadn't mentioned it."

Eliza frowned. "It doesn't make it right, but I can understand that. Did he speak to Mr Hobson at all?"

"He said that as soon as he saw him on his way to the maze, he bent down behind some blackcurrant bushes. He had no desire to talk to him, but Mr Hobson had already seen him. In Mr Turner's words, 'Mr Hobson made a point of showing off in his fancy new suit while I–' that's Mr Turner '– was in my dirty gardening clothes.'"

"That must have been difficult."

"Mr Turner said that in that moment, he realised it was Mr Hobson who had been behind the burglary. Not only because of the way he spoke, but because there was no chance he could afford the suit he was wearing on a foreman's wage."

"And he'd tried to blame Mr Turner? That's terrible."

The inspector sighed. "That was Mr Turner's opinion too. He also said that once the police dropped the case against him, they didn't reopen it. He'd never understood why, but it suddenly dawned on him that if Mr Hobson was the one pushing for the conviction, he wasn't going to pursue it if he was the guilty party."

"Surely they should have done that ... or at least the owner of the workshop."

"You'd have thought so, but clearly there was something going on. Anyway, when Mr Turner saw Mr Hobson on Saturday morning, he decided he wanted to make things right."

"So he *did* go after him?"

Inspector Adams nodded. "He said he'd followed him as far as the maze, but when he wasn't by the entrance, he went back to his gardening."

Eliza cocked her head to one side. "He didn't follow him inside?"

"He said not."

"And you believe him?"

"To tell you the truth, I didn't. I was even considering Sergeant Cooper's demands to arrest him."

"So what changed your mind?"

"He told us he'd spotted Mr Swift walking to the maze after he'd returned to the garden."

"Which would mean he had an alibi for the time of the murder."

"Precisely."

Eliza tapped her fingers on the varnished wood of the counter. "This Mr Swift, why do I feel so uncomfortable about him?" She studied the floor, her mind whirling, but a second later she lifted her eyes to meet the inspector's. "Mr Turner must have known him if he visited the workshop."

"He did, he admitted as much to us, although he said that whenever Mr Swift called, he and Mr Hobson always stepped outside, so he's no idea what their business was about."

"So that matches what the men in the workshop told you, but Mr Turner said he didn't recognise Mr Swift. I suppose that if the only reason he'd seen him before was because of Mr Hobson, it explains why he didn't want to admit it."

Inspector Adams reached for the hat he'd placed on the end of the counter. "You're right. There still has to be suspicion surrounding Mr Turner, but at the moment it's not convincing enough to arrest him."

"What will you do now?"

"We need to find this Mr Swift. He seems to be central to everything, but nobody knows anything about him. Sergeant Cooper and I will travel to Molesey this afternoon to see if we can find out any more."

"Very well." Eliza paused. "Don't forget about the brother too. He must be somewhere."

Inspector Adams raised his hat. "Leave it with us, Mrs Thomson. We'll keep up the search until we find them."

Archie was on his way to luncheon when he popped his head into the dispensary. "You're still here. I expected you to have gone through for luncheon."

Eliza was roused from her thoughts. "Yes, I'm just going."

"So what's troubling you?"

Eliza spoke as they walked down the hall and into the dining room. "Inspector Adams saw Mr Turner earlier, and it turns out that not only did he work with Mr Hobson, but he recognised Mr Swift as well."

"But he told you he knew neither of them?"

"Exactly, and I believed him. That's what's troubling me."

Archie put a hand on her shoulder. "You can't be right all the time. Don't let it worry you."

"You took your time." Henry was waiting at the table with his grandfather. "The gong sounded five minutes ago."

"I'm sorry, but I'm trying to work out who this Mr Swift

is. It might help if we understand why he called on Mr Hobson so regularly. I don't get the impression they were friends, more like business acquaintances."

Henry helped himself to a slice of bread and butter as the maid delivered four bowls of soup. "Did Inspector Adams go to the palace this morning?"

"He did, but other than finding out that Mr Turner was being less than honest with us, he didn't learn much more. I need to go over there again this afternoon."

Archie dropped his spoon. "What on earth for?"

"Because the police don't have a woman's intuition. I'm sure they're missing something, and unless I talk to Mr Turner directly, I shan't believe he's told us everything he knows."

Henry sat up straight. "I'll escort you; I'm guessing Mrs Appleton won't be joining you."

Eliza's shoulders slumped. "Oh goodness, I'd forgotten about that. She won't come unless she has permission from Sergeant Cooper."

Archie gave her a sideways glance. "Since when did I ever have that effect on you!"

Eliza's eyes narrowed. "That's a very good point. If there's any future in that relationship, Connie needs to start as she means to go on."

Mr Bell laughed. "I'm not sure that's what Archie meant."

"Maybe not, but it's about time Connie stood up for herself."

Henry grinned. "Can I still escort you, though?"

"Of course. As soon as we've finished here, I'll go and tell Connie she's coming with us, and I won't take no for an answer."

Connie had already tidied up after luncheon and was

sitting by the fire with a pile of mending when Eliza walked in.

"I hope you're not planning on finishing all that today." Eliza nodded at the clothes.

"Oh, I wish. I've been putting it off for so long, it will take me hours to get through." She fastened off the button she was sewing onto a blouse and stood up to hang it over the back of a chair. "Why?"

"We need to go over to Hampton Court Palace again. Inspector Adams spoke to Mr Turner this morning, and he admitted to knowing Mr Hobson and Mr Swift, but I've a feeling we're missing something."

Connie hesitated. "I don't know…"

"You don't know what?"

"Whether I should or not."

Eliza cocked her head to one side. "Why? We always do things together. You're not abandoning me, are you?"

"No, of course not, but I do have to think of Sergeant Cooper."

Eliza shook her head. "Why do you? You've only been on one official outing with him. That's no reason to change your whole life."

"But what if I upset him?"

"If you do, then he's not the man we think he is." Eliza softened her tone when she noticed Connie's shoulders sag. "Not that I think he will be. He knows we often go out together in the afternoon."

Connie slumped back into her chair. "Going out for a walk around the village is one thing, but interfering with an enquiry…"

"We are not interfering." Eliza took a deep breath. "We're

helping, and if we want to go to the palace again, why shouldn't we? If we happen to bump into Mr Turner, it would be purely coincidental. Now, will you please put that sewing away and get your hat and coat? I've asked for the carriage to be ready for quarter past one, and I'd like you to be in it."

Fifteen minutes in the carriage hadn't been long enough for Connie to relax, and as they pulled up in front of the palace, she tightened her grip on her handbag.

"You're sure Sergeant Cooper won't be visiting here this afternoon?"

"Positive. I told you, they're going to Molesey ... and even if he is here, it doesn't matter. You don't have to get his permission for everything. You're not married yet."

"Eliza! That's rather premature. We may never be." Connie's cheeks coloured. "It just seems wrong."

"Oh, Connie, it shouldn't. This is 1903. Women are fighting for the vote, you shouldn't need approval to go out with your best friend."

"I suppose so."

Once they were out of the carriage, Henry ushered them to the left of the main entrance, to the path that ran along the side of the walled gardens. Eliza peered in the direction of the kitchen garden.

"I hope Mr Turner's working in the same place. We could be hours looking for him otherwise."

"You mean we're deliberately going to see him, rather than visiting the palace?"

"We're going to walk around the gardens first and we'll go inside later, if we get time. Don't be so worried."

The path alongside the walled gardens was quiet once

they passed through the gate, and Eliza admired the colours of the late summer plants as they bloomed in the borders.

"I suppose he could be in any of these." Henry peered through the door of the first one. "There's someone in here; what does this Mr Turner look like?"

"He's tall and slim, with dark hair. Blue eyes, if you get close enough."

Henry stepped back. "That's not him then. He's got grey hair. Shall we keep going?"

It was as they reached the third garden that Henry stopped and beckoned Eliza forward.

"Is that him?"

"It is, and thankfully he's on his own." Eliza flashed Henry a smile. "Come along, let's find out what he has to say for himself." She led the way between the raised beds stocked to overflowing with fruit bushes. "Good afternoon, Mr Turner."

The gardener jumped backwards when he saw them. "I've already spoken to the police; I've nothing more to say."

Eliza held up her hands. "Please, we haven't come to accuse you of anything. We're aware you've spoken to Inspector Adams and also that you knew Mr Hobson and Mr Swift. The thing is, I have a feeling you know more about the murder than you realise."

His eyes shifted as he stepped back. "What do you mean?"

"Well, for a start, I'm particularly interested in the relationship between the two men. I understand Mr Swift visited the workshop roughly once a month. Do you have any idea what it was about?"

"No, as I said to the police, they always stepped outside."

"But you think it was more of a business arrangement rather than a friendship?"

"Oh yes, I would say so. He'd usually call at about four o'clock in the afternoon and only stay for a couple of minutes."

"That's a strange time to call."

"I suppose it is. He always reminded me of a bank manager or something like that, and so I assumed he called once the branch was closed. I never saw Mr Hobson with him at any other time."

"But did you see him around Molesey, when you visited the bank, for example?"

"Oh, he wasn't from Molesey. I couldn't say where he was from, but not around here."

"So how would Mr Hobson know him, given he lived and worked in the village?"

Mr Turner shrugged. "He was in London before he came causing trouble around here. He may have been one of his acquaintances from there."

"I suppose that's possible. Did Mr Hobson ever travel back to London?"

"I don't think so. The rest of us in the workshop used to joke that he'd come down here to hide, but now I'm not so sure it wasn't true. To my knowledge, the furthest he ever travelled was Kingston."

"He'd go to Kingston?" Eliza looked at Connie and Henry, while Mr Turner clipped a dying side shoot from an apple tree.

"I've no idea how I know this, but I've a feeling he banked there."

"Oh my goodness!" Eliza stared at Connie. "You realise what this means, don't you?"

Connie shook her head, confusion etched across her face, but Henry grinned as Eliza turned back to Mr Turner.

"I presume you'd recognise Mr Swift if you saw him again?" Her voice quivered.

"I certainly would ... and I apologise for telling you I didn't know him..."

"Let's not dwell on that for the moment." Eliza took out her notepad. "I've a feeling you may be able to help us identify this Mr Swift."

"Me?" Mr Turner scanned the gardens. "Why, is he here?"

"No, but I suspect I know where he is. Would you be free to visit us in Moreton-on-Thames on Sunday morning?"

"I'm not sure ... it's a long way to travel..."

"Of course, but don't worry about getting a carriage; we'll arrange one for you."

Mr Turner failed to be convinced. "I ... erm ... I usually go to church. Could we make it another time?"

"You're a churchgoer? Splendid. I'd hoped you'd be able to join us for the service in Moreton."

"You want me to go to church with you?"

Eliza smiled. "Don't look so worried. I've nothing sinister planned. But if you could be with us for ten o'clock, I'd be much obliged. There's someone I'd like you to meet. You're also welcome to stay for Sunday luncheon. My husband and father will be there too."

Henry nodded as the man's eyes flicked towards him.

"All right, I suppose so. I'll see you then."

## CHAPTER THIRTEEN

The surgery was unusually quiet on Friday morning, which allowed Eliza time to dust around the bottles on the shelves. As she reached the shelf of coloured jars, the door swung open and Connie burst in.

"What on earth's the matter?"

The red rims of Connie's eyes suggested she'd been crying. "Sergeant Cooper's cross with me."

"Why? How do you know?"

"He called this morning to say he'd missed seeing me yesterday, and when I told him we'd been to Hampton Court, well ... his face dropped. I could tell he was angry, and he said we should leave the investigation to him and Inspector Adams."

"Oh, my dear." Eliza extended her arms and sat Connie on a chair. "I doubt he was mad with you for going to the palace. Did you tell him we'd walked around the state rooms?"

Connie shook her head. "How could I when I felt like a naughty child?"

"I'm sure he wasn't cross with you, but the police get

rather protective about their job. I presume you didn't mention anything about our conversation with Mr Turner?"

Connie sobbed. "I didn't want to upset him any further. Oh, Eliza, I wish I hadn't gone with you."

"Come on now, don't be silly. Just because you're walking out together, doesn't mean he can control everything you do. You need to start as you mean to go on. It will make life easier in the long run."

"But what if he doesn't want that? What if he won't see me again if I carry on like this? After everything we've gone through to get to this stage."

Eliza sat back and studied her friend. "Shall I tell you what I think?" When Connie agreed, she continued. "That you'd be better off without him if he expects you to ask permission every time you want to go out."

"But that's how it was..."

"With Mr Appleton maybe, but that was over five years ago and things are changing. Take me and Archie..."

"But you're different. You're so clever and Dr Thomson doesn't mind when you make your own decisions."

"Only because I don't let him. It's not that he cares for me any less, but he knows what's important to me ... and surely our friendship is worth standing up to Sergeant Cooper for?"

A look of recognition crossed Connie's face. "You're right! Saying I shouldn't have gone to the palace wasn't any different to telling me I couldn't go out with my friend. He can't do that... Not when he's at work, anyway."

Eliza smiled. "And you know what, he'll probably think more of you for it, not less. Now cheer up. We need to visit Mrs Petty this afternoon. I promised to report back if we found out who the accused man was. I also want to update her about Mr Swift."

"Will you tell her you think it's really Mr King?" Connie's eyes widened.

"I might. She picks up so much sitting in that window, I'd like to see if she has anything to add before Mr Turner arrives on Sunday. I'll meet you here at one."

The sun bobbed in and out of the clouds as Eliza and Connie walked across the green to Mrs Petty's. She was waiting at the front door when they arrived.

"I hoped you were coming here." She ushered them to their usual seats by the window. "I put the kettle on, just in case. Shall I make some tea?"

"Yes, that would be lovely, thank you."

With the tea made and the tray on the table, Mrs Petty sat down.

"Did you find what you were looking for at the library?"

Eliza smiled. "We did, thank you. I'm sorry we couldn't come and tell you about it yesterday, but we had a sudden need to go back to the palace."

"Ooh, that sounds interesting. Why?"

"We found out that the accused man, the one whose name you couldn't recall, was called Mr Turner. The trial was actually held in January of this year, but even though he was found not guilty, he lost his job at the workshop."

Mrs Petty's smile brightened. "He got a position at the palace, didn't he? Was it in the gardens?"

"My word, Mrs Petty, how do you remember these things?" Connie's mouth dropped open.

Mrs Petty chuckled. "I've plenty of time to read in the mornings before the villagers are out and about, and I like to know what's going on. Did he see what happened at the maze?"

"That's what we needed to find out. He originally told us he'd never seen the victim or the man who followed him, but as soon as we found out he was the one Mr Hobson had accused of burglary, we knew he was lying."

Mrs Petty shook her head. "I should have remembered. It would have saved you so much time."

"Mrs Petty! If it wasn't for you, we wouldn't even have known about the trial. You've already been a great help, but I do have another question for you. How well acquainted are you with Mr King?"

"You mean the grumpy man who went with us to the palace, but didn't travel back?"

"That's the one."

"Not very, I'm afraid. I believe he's a bank manager in Kingston, and they moved here from London, but that's about it. The bottom of my garden only just reaches the boundary of his, and so it's difficult to overhear anything." Mrs Petty sighed. "More's the pity."

"Hmm. Have you any idea what time he goes to work in the morning and when he gets home each evening?"

"He's as regular as clockwork when he goes out. He leaves here at eight o'clock prompt. As soon as the church clock starts to strike."

"And what about coming home?"

Mrs Petty put a finger to her chin. "He's back by four o'clock most days, although occasionally it's closer to half past four. He picks the children up from school."

Eliza sat up straight. "Who takes them?"

"They leave with him too. I imagine they go somewhere in Kingston."

"Do you ever see them going out as a family? With the mother as well?"

Mrs Petty shook her head. "No, never. I was rather surprised they all came with us on Saturday."

"That's strange, Dr Thomson was too, although I never asked him why. Do you ever speak to Mrs King while he's at work?"

"I can't say I do. Before Saturday, the only time I'd seen her was in the garden." Mrs Petty paused. "And she never has visitors. That can't be right, can it?"

"No, it can't." Connie's voice was strong. "She needs her own friends. Perhaps we should ask her to join us for afternoon tea."

Eliza beamed at her friend. "What a splendid idea. We should have done it sooner to welcome her to the village. We could call on our way home and invite her to the surgery tomorrow."

"All to find out about her husband?" Mrs Petty's eyes narrowed.

Eliza laughed. "That's not the only reason, but can you think of a better way?"

With a final farewell to Mrs Petty, Eliza and Connie turned into the cul-de-sac that ran down the side of her garden and walked up the path of the second house on the right. Despite the sun shining on the back of the house, all the curtains were pulled across the front windows.

"Do you think that's to stop prying eyes?"

Connie glanced to the sky. "Well, it isn't to keep out the sun."

"Let's see what she's up to then." Eliza rapped on the door-knocker and the two of them stepped back, waiting for the door to open. When it didn't, they tried again.

Connie contemplated the house. "Maybe it's the maid's half day."

"She should still be capable of answering the door herself."

"What if she takes an afternoon nap?"

Eliza put her hands on her hips. "If she does, let's try waking her up."

This time the hammering on the door did the trick, and a minute later Mrs King, immaculately dressed in a fitted lilac dress with matching hat, glared out at them.

"Ah, Mrs King." Eliza gave her best smile. "I'm sorry to disturb you if you're about to go out, but we realised on Saturday that we hadn't been properly introduced. We wondered if you'd like to join us at the surgery for afternoon tea..."

"No. I won't be able to." Mrs King began to close the door, but Eliza reached out her hand to keep it open.

"I'm sorry, you misunderstand; I was thinking of one day next week."

"The day of the week doesn't matter. I need to be here for when my husband comes home."

"Of course, I was forgetting. He arrives home early, doesn't he?"

"He has his routine."

Eliza gave a polite smile. "Don't we all. Would you prefer to join us for morning coffee instead?"

Mrs King's frame was rigid. "No, I think not. He'd rather I didn't leave the house."

Eliza's face clearly changed.

"I mean, he likes me to be home in case of unexpected visitors ... or deliveries ... and we have such a lovely house."

"It must have been nice to go out for the day last Saturday then. I saw you admiring the Fountain Garden when we were leaving the palace."

"Yes, it was delightful."

For a moment Eliza thought Mrs King's face was softening, but a glaze immediately returned to her eyes.

"It's a shame you had to leave so suddenly. Did you see any more of the grounds?"

"Like the Pond Garden? That was a lovely spot." Connie's voice had an innocence Eliza could never manage.

"No, we left via the Lion Gate, and so we only saw that part of the garden as we walked through. Now, if you'll excuse me, my husband will be home shortly."

Before Eliza could respond, the door shut in their faces. She stared at Connie but was unable to speak as they walked down the path.

"Did that really happen?" She couldn't keep the incredulity from her voice. "She stays in all day, every day, because he doesn't want her going out?"

"I imagine that's why they have such an immaculate house. To keep her happy."

"It's more like a gilded prison." Eliza couldn't disguise the anger in her voice.

Connie squeezed her arm. "Cheer up. It looks as if he's taking her out somewhere nice tonight, judging by her outfit."

"That's neither here nor there. If you ask me, he's told her to stay in, and despite the fact she knows he won't be home until four o'clock, she's too frightened to disobey him."

Connie shuddered. "He was rather stern when Dr Thomson tried to talk to him on Saturday morning."

"He was, and somehow I can't help thinking he's involved with this murder."

"But how could he be?"

Eliza smiled. "I'm hoping we'll begin answering that on Sunday."

As they reached the corner of the cul-de-sac, Eliza stepped into the road to cross over to the village green, but was held back as Connie stopped and looked to her right.

"Would you like to walk home the long way around?"

Connie's cheeks coloured. "Would you mind?"

Eliza returned to the footpath. "Come along. If Sergeant Cooper's anything like you, he'll be stood outside the station wondering where you are."

"Don't be silly, he has work to do."

"I'll still wager we'll find him outside, but even if he isn't, do you want to call in?"

Connie sighed. "I'd like to speak to him, to make sure he's not still angry with me, but we can't tell him we've been to visit Mrs King."

"Why not? It was a perfectly normal afternoon, visiting two neighbours. You don't want to be like Mrs King, do you? Frightened to leave the house."

"No, I don't! She takes things too far."

"Well, be careful then."

They rounded the bend in the road that brought the police station into view.

"What did I tell you?" Eliza nudged Connie when she saw Sergeant Cooper leaning against the door frame. "He's probably been as distressed as you about this morning, so I suggest you make the most of it. Let him know that you won't always be chained to the house."

The sergeant's face lit up as soon as he spotted them. "Mrs Appleton, I was hoping you'd walk this way."

Connie smiled. "We took the long way round. We've been to visit Mrs Petty and called in on Mrs King while we were there."

"You visited Mrs King?" The sergeant's brow creased.

Eliza nodded. "It was long overdue, Sergeant. We like to welcome newcomers to the village, but somehow we missed her out."

"Not that she wanted welcoming." A scowl crossed Connie's face. "Can you believe she declined our offer of afternoon tea?"

Sergeant Cooper cleared his throat. "She may have been busy preparing for her husband coming home. Don't ladies do things like that?"

Connie shook her head. "She was more than ready, judging by the dress she was wearing. No, by the sound of it, she stays in because Mr King doesn't want her to go out." She gave the sergeant an indignant look. "Can you imagine that? All I can say is that it's a good job he isn't married to either of us." She turned to Eliza. "We wouldn't put up with anything like that, would we, Mrs Thomson?"

Eliza grinned. "No, my dear Mrs Appleton, we most certainly would not."

## CHAPTER FOURTEEN

Eliza lay in bed listening to the sound of the birds. With no surgery or church to attend, she always enjoyed Saturday morning. It was the one day of the week she could doze for an extra half an hour. Not that she should this morning. With everything that had happened over the last few days, she was behind with her paperwork; but that could wait. Another ten minutes wouldn't hurt.

Breakfast was always at nine o'clock at the weekend, and so by the time she reached the dining room, the men were already at the table. They glanced up as she arrived.

"I was about to come and look for you. What have you been doing?" Archie bit into a slice of toast and marmalade.

"Taking my time; is that a crime?"

"Only when it stops the rest of us having breakfast." Henry smirked at her as she sat down.

"You all carry on. You always eat more than I do, anyway."

Mr Bell reached for his cup of tea. "What do you have planned for today?"

"Nothing much. I need to put in a few orders for the surgery and want to see if the newspaper has any more details of the murder. Other than that, my time's my own. Are you and Archie going to the bowling club this afternoon?"

"We are, there's a match on. Why don't you come and watch us?"

Eliza turned to the window to see wisps of clouds in the sky. "I might do that. It's always a pleasant way to pass the time. At least then Connie will be close to Sergeant Cooper too."

Henry laughed. "It seems strange seeing them together. Aren't they too old to be walking out with each other?"

Eliza scowled. "Of course they're not. Mrs Appleton especially is in the prime of her life. Anyway, what are you doing today?"

Henry shrugged. "Not a lot. I'll be in the Golden Eagle after luncheon, but who knows, I may join you to watch the bowls. It depends on the company in the bar."

Eliza's eyes bored into him. "You're spending far too much time in there. I can see it's time you were starting work. At least you've not got long to go now."

Henry smiled. "And I'll be back in London again too. I must admit I'm looking forward to it."

"Well, if you're at a loose end this morning, you can help me with the orders, and I'll take them to the post office this afternoon when I go out."

Henry grimaced. "What about helping you with the murder investigation instead? Aren't you working on it any more?"

Eliza sighed. "We are, but we're at something of a dead end until tomorrow."

Archie lowered the newspaper he was reading. "What's happening tomorrow?"

"Ah, I forgot to tell you." Eliza kept her head down as she scraped butter over a piece of toast. "I've invited over Mr Turner, the gardener from the palace."

"Why?"

She now had Archie's full attention.

"Because he was one of the few people who saw this Mr Swift, and I want to ask him about him." Eliza stood up to pour a cup of tea as Archie's eyes bored into her.

"You were at the palace the other day and had every opportunity to speak to him then. Why does he need to come here?"

Eliza pursed her lips as she placed the knife on her plate. "I've invited him to church ... and to join us for luncheon."

"For goodness' sake." Archie slammed his napkin onto the table, but Mr Bell held up a hand.

"She may have her reasons; let her speak."

"It's only a hunch, but I want to check whether this *Mr Swift* lives in Moreton."

"I've told you, he doesn't. I'm the family doctor in this village and there isn't anyone called Swift on my records."

"But I'd like to make sure. Is it so wrong to invite him?"

"Yes, actually, it is." Archie stood up and paced to the window. "We know he was near the maze around the time of the murder. How can we be certain it wasn't him with the knife?"

"He has an alibi..."

"From someone who wasn't paying enough attention to realise he'd gone missing for five minutes." He banged a hand to his head. "You know as well as I do that the gardeners must be high on the list of suspects. They can almost certainly make their way around the maze better than anyone else, and you have to admit Mr Turner had a pretty solid motive."

"Maybe he did, but I happen to believe he's innocent. If he'd wanted Mr Hobson dead, he would have done it outside his place of work. It's too obvious."

"And is that why you've discounted the other gardeners?"

"We've spoken to them all and as far as we're aware, none of them had a motive."

"That's what Mr Turner told you to start with…"

Henry raised his eyebrows. "Why don't we ask Mr Turner about them tomorrow? If the man's coming for luncheon, he can at least tell us a bit more about the men he works with."

Eliza let out a sigh. "Thank you. I was thinking the same thing. We'll find out about the workings of the palace without making him feel under any pressure." She looked to Archie, who was still eying her. "You will be nice to him, won't you?"

"Do I have any choice?"

Eliza was early calling for Connie and she took a seat in her friend's small but neat living room as Connie fixed her hat.

"Archie wasn't pleased I'd invited Mr Turner for luncheon."

"I wondered how he'd react. What did you tell him?"

"Only that we wanted to check whether there was a Mr Swift in Moreton. He immediately told me there wasn't, of course, so I just hope Mr Turner makes the connection between Mr Swift and Mr King."

"You didn't mention your suspicions?"

Eliza huffed. "He didn't give me a chance. Henry saved

me by suggesting we ask Mr Turner about the other gardeners at the palace and find out whether they had a motive."

Connie turned back from the mirror. "Weren't you going to do that, anyway?"

"I was, but I was glad of the diversion. The one thing we probably won't get much help with though is the murder weapon. It's been forgotten in all the discussions, but someone must have carried it from the maze to the Pond Garden."

"And from the kitchen to the maze." Connie's forehead creased. "Mr Swift must have had something to do with that, surely?"

"You would think so, as long as he's our killer. It's back to the drawing board if he's not."

Connie walked to the hall to fetch her coat. "Oh, I hope he is. We don't want to go back to square one."

The two of them left the house and walked past the surgery on their way to the bowling green. Eliza had several letters in her hand.

"I need to drop these at the post office on the way."

Connie grimaced. "It's to be hoped Mrs Pitt isn't behind the counter then."

"What do you mean?" Eliza stared at her until she recalled their last encounter. "Oh gracious, I'd completely forgotten, she wasn't happy with me when we came home on Saturday."

"I imagine she'll recover if you give her a bit of gossip. Only details you don't mind her passing on though." Connie chuckled. "I wouldn't trust her with a secret."

"I'll just tell her what we know so far. It isn't much, after all."

"Did you ever hear any more about the brother?"

# THE PALACE MURDER

"No, now you mention it, I didn't. I presume Inspector Adams hasn't found him, or he'd have called to let us know. Either that or Sergeant Cooper would have used it as an excuse to visit."

Connie's cheeks reddened. "He doesn't need much of an excuse to call any more."

Eliza laughed. "I expect you're right. It could be another question for Mr Turner, though. He worked with Mr Hobson and so he may know something about him."

"There's no harm in asking."

Connie pushed on the door of the small corner shop as they arrived, but hesitated as Mrs Pitt glared from behind the dark mahogany counter.

"Good afternoon, Mrs Pitt."

"Ladies." Mrs Pitt's gaze focused on Eliza. "I'm good enough to talk to now, I see."

Eliza forced back a sigh. "You always were, Mrs Pitt; I'm sorry for the way I behaved on Saturday. It had been a difficult day, and I needed time to think."

"Well, good manners cost nothing."

"No, you're right." She handed over her letters. "Will you forgive me and send these for Dr Thomson? I'm afraid we're out of stamps."

Mrs Pitt flicked through them. "I can manage that. Will you pay now or shall I put it on the account?"

"On account, please. They're for surgery business and so Dr Thomson will pay for them." Eliza flashed her best smile and was about to usher Connie to the door when Mrs Pitt stopped them.

"So ... did you work out who murdered the man in the maze?"

"No, I'm afraid we've not, although we have learned the name of the victim."

"Really?" Mrs Pitt's eyes were wide as she rested her hands on the counter. "Anyone I know?"

"It was a man called Gerard Hobson. He worked in Over Moreton for about five years, in the early 1870s. Were you in the village then?"

Mrs Pitt screwed up her face. "We were, but I can't say I remember anyone of that name."

"No, well, he went to London after he left here but was working in his home village of Molesey at the time of the incident."

"Ooh, so not far from the palace then. If anybody had a grudge, it would be easy to lure him to the maze and attack him ... I should imagine."

Eliza chuckled. "I imagine it would, although we're still trying to work out why anyone would want to do that."

Mrs Pitt shuddered. "I'm so glad we visited the royal kitchens first. If it hadn't been for one of the attendants pushing past us to get help, we'd have missed the whole thing."

"You should count yourself fortunate; it isn't a pleasant way to start the day."

"I'm sure it's not."

Eliza reached for Connie's arm. "Good day, Mrs Pitt."

## CHAPTER FIFTEEN

Eliza looked around the living room, satisfied it was in a suitable condition to receive guests. *Ten o'clock. He'll be here in a minute.* She hurried to the dining room where Archie sat finishing his cup of tea.

"Aren't you ready yet? Mr Turner will be here any time now."

"What's the rush? We don't leave for church for another quarter of an hour."

"That's as maybe, but I'd rather you didn't disappear as soon as he arrives." She peered out into the hall at the sound of footsteps on the stairs. "Father and Henry are here. It's only you we're waiting for."

"All right, I'll only be a minute."

Archie had no sooner disappeared than there was a knock on the front door.

"He's here!" Eliza ushered Mr Bell into the living room and waited while the maid received their visitor. A moment later, there was a tap on the door.

"Mr Turner for you, madam."

Eliza marvelled at how different he looked in his Sunday best suit, with his hair greased down. "Good morning, Mr Turner. I trust you had a pleasant journey."

"Yes, madam; thank you. It wasn't as far as I expected."

Eliza smiled. "I said exactly the same thing when we came to the palace last week. I'd no idea how close it was to Moreton." She turned to introduce Henry and Mr Bell. "They'll be joining us for church along with my husband, Dr Thomson. We'll meet my good friend Mrs Appleton once we're there."

Mr Turner gulped. "W-would you mind explaining why you wanted me to join you?"

"I'm sorry. I suppose I was rather cryptic the other day. The thing is, you said you'd recognise Mr Swift again, and I've a feeling he'll be at church this morning."

"Mr Swift will be?" Mr Bell's brows drew together. "Archie said…"

"I'm aware Dr Thomson doesn't have a Mr Swift on his list, but I can't help feeling he's here in Moreton. I'm hoping Mr Turner can prove me right."

"I'll try my best…" Mr Turner stopped as Archie joined them and offered him a hand.

"Good morning. I see my wife has you involved in one of her little investigations. She refuses to believe me when I tell her Mr Swift doesn't live around here."

Mr Turner stared at them, but Eliza patted him on the arm. "Take no notice; he just doesn't want to be proved wrong. Shall we go?"

Connie and Sergeant Cooper were waiting for them in the churchyard when they arrived, but Mr Turner froze as soon as he saw them.

"You've brought the police?"

Eliza chuckled at the sight of the sergeant, who looked rather dashing in his newly pressed uniform. "Oh, don't mind Sergeant Cooper. He and Mrs Appleton are walking out together. There's no more to it than that."

Mr Turner let out an audible sigh, but Sergeant Cooper stepped towards Eliza, the creases in his brow obvious.

"What's going on?"

"Ah, Sergeant Cooper, you remember Mr Turner?"

"Certainly, I do. He's a suspect in our murder investigation. What's he doing here?"

Eliza took the sergeant to one side. "Hopefully, we'll prove he's no such thing. He's one of the few people who can identify this Mr Swift we're after. I want to be sure he doesn't live in Moreton."

"We already know he doesn't."

"Please, Sergeant. I'd like to be sure." She glanced back to Mr Turner. "Would you mind if we go inside?"

The church was only half full as they entered, and with Connie sitting alongside Sergeant Cooper, there was room for Mr Turner to sit with Eliza at the back. She scrutinised those present as she leaned in close to him.

"It's still early yet, but do you see Mr Swift in the congregation?"

Mr Turner surveyed those in front of him until finally he shook his head. "No. The men with beards are generally too old or too short."

"That's what I thought." She peered towards the door that stood immediately to their right. "If he does come in, you needn't do anything other than point him out. We don't want to make a fuss."

Eliza sensed his tension easing.

"Very well; I doubt he'll recognise me, anyway."

Eliza studied the pews as they filled up with the regular attendees, but by the time the organ started for the first hymn, there was no sign of Mr Swift. *Should we take it as an indication of guilt if he misses church two weeks running?* She flicked through her hymn book to find the right page, but as the rest of the congregation burst into song, her attention wandered back to the door and the churchyard beyond it. *What do we do if he doesn't turn up?*

The vicar plodded through the service at his usual pace, but Eliza's mind was racing. She had to find Mr King, but short of knocking on his front door, she was at a loss. By the time the vicar climbed the steps of the ornately carved wooden pulpit, a smile crept across her lips. She had a plan.

As the service came to a close, Eliza again leaned towards Mr Turner. "I presume there's no sign of Mr Swift."

"No, madam; I'm sorry."

Eliza patted him on the arm. "There's no need to apologise; the man I believe to be Mr Swift isn't here, either, so we could still be talking about the same person. Not to worry, I've another idea."

She watched the vicar walk to the back of the church and once he reached the door, she turned to Archie. "We need to leave."

"What's the rush?"

"I'll tell you outside. Come along." She caught hold of his arm and with Mr Turner following them, she made her way past the vicar and into the churchyard.

"Now, where's Connie? We'll have to wait for her." She directed Mr Turner away from the door, shuddering as the sun disappeared behind a large cloud. "Gosh, it's gone cool out here. I should have brought my thicker coat. Still, a brisk walk will warm us up."

Archie's eyes narrowed. "Does this walk involve going further than the surgery?"

"I thought it would be nice to show Mr Turner the village. We can take the long way home."

Mr Turner shrivelled under Archie's stare. "I don't mind going straight back to the surgery."

"Nonsense, Mr Turner." Eliza nudged him on the arm. "I doubt you'll be coming to Moreton again, so let me give you a guided tour. There's a rather nice duck pond at the far end."

Archie raised his eyebrows. "How long will this take you?"

Eliza shook her head at Mr Turner. "Take no notice of him, he's only thinking of his stomach."

"I'm sure Mr Turner would like to eat too."

"And so we shall, as soon as Connie appears and we've taken a walk. I expect Sergeant Cooper will need to get back to the station."

As the minutes passed, Eliza began to wonder if her friend had gone without her, but finally, as the church clock struck noon, Connie appeared on the arm of Sergeant Cooper.

"Here you are." A wave of relief washed over Eliza. "What have you been doing?"

Connie's cheeks flushed. "I'm sorry, but so many people wanted to comment on me being with Sergeant Cooper, I got a bit waylaid."

"Of course, it's the first time you've attended church together. I hope everyone's happy for you."

"Oh, yes." She gave the sergeant a sideways glance as she leaned towards Eliza. "I think he was rather flattered by all the comments."

"I imagine they went something along the lines of 'What a fortunate man you are, Sergeant.'"

The colour in Connie's cheeks deepened. "Something like that. Anyway, what did you want?"

"We're taking Mr Turner for a tour of the village. We'll walk with Sergeant Cooper as far as the station, and Henry has said he'll escort us the rest of the way. We'd better hurry though, before everyone settles down for luncheon."

"What do you mean?" Connie's brow creased, until a look of recognition crossed her face. "Ah, I know."

They left the churchyard as a group, but as Archie and Mr Bell headed towards the surgery, Mr Turner stopped to watch them.

"I can't help thinking your husband doesn't trust me."

"He's fine. He'd have come with us if he really didn't like you."

As predicted, Sergeant Cooper walked with them as far as the police station, after which their first point of interest was the public house.

"The Golden Eagle. Not a bad place for a game of cards or dominos." Henry glanced at Eliza. "Do you want us to see if Mr Swift's in there? If it's the man you think it is, he often is."

"I don't want you staying for a drink..." She hesitated. "Although, I suppose you could pop your head in to check."

"Oh, nobody will think that's suspicious."

Eliza shrugged. "It needn't, if you do it casually. If anyone asks, tell them you're looking for someone else ... one of your friends."

"Very well." Henry grimaced as he held the door open for Mr Turner. They hadn't been gone a minute when they were back. "No. No sign of him."

Eliza released her breath. "Never mind. It was a good try. Shall we carry on?"

Henry walked with Mr Turner as he followed his mother. "Does Molesey have a decent boozer?"

"It's quite pleasant; not that I go in any more. Not since the trial."

Eliza cocked her head to one side. "Why not? You did nothing wrong."

"People still talk and I can do without it to be honest. Especially after Mr Hobson's death. I imagine they all have me down as the murderer."

"That's terrible." Connie studied their guest. "What happened to a man being innocent until proven guilty?"

"What indeed. Unfortunately, in a place like Molesey, they act as the judge and jury without hearing the evidence."

Eliza sighed. "There are people like that everywhere. As you can see though, Moreton-on-Thames is smaller than Molesey and so we don't do too badly." She gestured towards the village green. "It probably helps that most of the houses are visible from almost anywhere. One of the few exceptions is this cul-de-sac." She guided the party around the corner to where several larger properties stood back from the road.

Mr Turner smiled. "Very nice. I don't suppose people with the money to buy these houses would want to be overlooked." He suddenly froze, and Eliza followed his gaze to see a man storm from the second house on the right. "That's him!"

Eliza started as Mr King marched down the drive and charged past them without a word. They all watched as he turned right out of the cul-de-sac and disappeared.

"I knew it!" A smile lit up Eliza's face. "Mr Swift and Mr King are one and the same man."

Connie clapped her hands in front of her chest. "Eliza, you're so clever."

Henry smirked as he nodded after him. "He'll be going to the Eagle."

"How do you know?"

"I told you, I often see him in there. Do you want us to go after him?"

"No, I don't." Eliza's brow creased. "We need to think about this ... and we'd better go for luncheon before your father comes looking for us." She linked Connie's arm and set off towards the village green. "Are you coming, Mr Turner?"

"What about the duck pond?"

"The what?" Eliza glanced back at him. "Oh, that, it's nothing really. You'll see it on your way out."

## CHAPTER SIXTEEN

Archie had a tray of sherries waiting for them when they arrived back at the surgery.

"That was quick. I wasn't expecting you for another twenty minutes."

"Thankfully, we came across the man in question and Mr Turner identified him as Mr Swift."

Archie's eyes narrowed as he handed Eliza a glass. "Mr Swift was in Moreton?"

A smirk crossed her lips. "He was, and not only that, he lives here. The reason you've no record of him is because you know him as Mr King."

"Mr King?" He stared at Mr Turner. "You're sure?"

"I'm positive. I saw him regularly when I was still at the workshop and I immediately recognised him at the maze last week."

Henry wandered over to his mother. "He's obviously up to no good if he uses an alias."

"My thoughts exactly." Eliza considered the idea. "You

said he goes into the Golden Eagle most evenings. What does he do?"

Henry shrugged. "Not a lot, really. He spends most of his time sitting at the bar watching everyone else enjoying themselves."

Connie cradled her sherry in front of her. "Do you remember him being in there on Friday evening by any chance?"

"The Friday just gone?" Henry only paused for a second. "Oh goodness, yes he was, and he was in a terrible mood. He had a right go at the bartender when he refused him another drink."

"What time was that?" Eliza asked.

Henry puffed out his cheeks. "He was in there when I arrived at seven o'clock and he ended up leaving before last orders, probably about ten."

Eliza looked at Connie. "That was the day we visited Mrs King."

"When we decided she was dressed up, ready to go out."

"Precisely, but she clearly wasn't ... unless they had a change of plan."

Connie put a hand to her chest. "You don't suppose she puts her best clothes on for him every evening, do you?"

Archie stepped between them. "When you two have quite finished, may I remind you we have a visitor?"

"My dear Mr Turner, I do apologise." Eliza waited as the gong sounded for luncheon. "Shall we go through to the dining room? We can talk more in there."

With Archie and Mr Bell seated at either end of the table, Eliza and Connie took their seats opposite Henry and Mr Turner. Their guest appeared apprehensive at the array of cutlery, and Eliza was thankful they were having soup to start. At least that made the order of use more obvious.

She waited for the maid to bring in the tureen and serve out six bowls before she spoke.

"Tell me, Mr Turner. How well did you know Mr Hobson?"

"He was an acquaintance, that's all. We did the work we needed to do, but that was it."

"Have you any idea why he blamed you for the theft?"

He shook his head. "I've spent many a sleepless night contemplating that, but I haven't come up with a single reason why he'd take such a dislike to me."

"There has to be a reason." Mr Bell let his spoon clang on the side of his bowl. "I know what it's like to be wrongly accused. There must have been some malice in it."

"Well, whatever it was, we won't find out now." Mr Turner's shoulders slumped. "I don't remember upsetting him enough to warrant such treatment."

Eliza rested her spoon in her empty bowl. "Did Mr Hobson ever mention a brother?"

Mr Turner laid down his own spoon as his forehead creased. "Not to me, although thinking about it, I did overhear him talking about him one day."

"Really? What did he say?"

"I don't recall. He was with someone I couldn't see, but it sounded as if his brother had upset him. He was having a right moan, telling this stranger how much he disliked him, but he stopped as soon as he saw me."

"That's interesting. Was this before or after he accused you of the theft?"

"Before. Why?"

Eliza studied him. "Could you have overheard something that was confidential?"

Mr Turner shrugged. "I don't think I did."

"It's only a thought, but maybe he was talking in confidence and assumed you overheard him. It may have been the reason he wanted you out of the way."

"Possibly, I never considered that."

Eliza sighed. "As you said, I don't suppose we ever will know for sure, unless you've any inkling of who he might have been talking to."

"No, none. He was outside and whoever he was with was in a carriage."

"Could it have been Mr King?" Archie raised his eyebrows. "If he was a regular visitor to the workshop, and they always met outside…"

"That's what I'm thinking." Eliza shot Mr Turner a glance. "Could that have been the case?"

"I suppose it could, but I couldn't confirm it. As I said, I didn't see the man and Mr Hobson was doing the talking."

Eliza turned to Archie. "It sounds like we need another chat with our unfriendly neighbour."

Archie shook his head. "You can count me out … and I don't think you should go either. It did you no good last time and Inspector Adams won't be pleased."

Eliza pouted. "You're probably right."

"Well, what about the other gardeners?" Connie sat back as the maid collected their bowls. "Mr Turner, you said you were in the same garden as Mr Clark when Mr Hobson walked past you. Was he there for the whole time?"

"Erm … yes."

"You don't seem sure." Eliza stared at him.

"He was there whenever I looked over."

"But you weren't there all the time?"

"I was ... except for when I slipped out to get my…"

Eliza put up a hand to stop him. "Except for when you followed Mr Hobson to the maze, you mean. Inspector Adams mentioned it to us."

"All right, yes." Mr Turner played with his dessert spoon. "I didn't go in, though. I swear. I told him that too."

"But could Mr Clark have left the garden while you were missing?" Henry's eyes were wide as he leaned forward over the table. "Is there any reason to think he was acquainted with Mr Hobson?"

"I couldn't say. He usually keeps himself to himself and doesn't talk much."

"Does he live in Molesey?" Connie asked. "I imagine he'd be familiar with Mr Hobson if he does."

Mr Turner shook his head. "No, actually he's from Kingston."

Eliza's head shot up, but she paused while the maid placed a large joint of roast beef on the table and passed Archie the carving knife and fork. He sliced the meat effortlessly, and with the plates handed around and subsequently filled with vegetables, the maid left them.

Eliza waited until everyone's plates were empty before she continued her questions. "Can you tell us about Mr Boyle? He was trimming the hedge at the side of the maze when the murder took place. Do you know where he lives?"

Mr Turner wiped a piece of Yorkshire pudding around his plate. "He's in Molesey, but I doubt he saw anything. He focuses on nothing but his work."

Eliza smiled. "He did see Mr Hobson and Mr Swift, as it happens, not that he could tell us much about them."

"That doesn't surprise me."

"What about the other man we saw?" Connie looked at Eliza. "Was it Mr Marshall?"

"Yes, the garden attendant. Would he be familiar with the maze?"

"I couldn't say for certain, but I imagine so. From what I understand, he's worked at the palace for years."

"Didn't he say he'd seen Mr Hobson arriving at the maze and Mr King in the Fountain Garden?" Archie placed his knife and fork side by side on the front of his plate. "He couldn't have done that if he was on the inside; he must have been on the path."

"You're right." Eliza slumped back in her chair, but her eyes narrowed as she studied Mr Turner. "Did you see him when you were at the maze?"

Mr Turner shook his head. "No, I don't think so."

"But you said you were there before Mr Hobson and Mr King."

"Yes."

"In which case you should have seen Mr Marshall."

Mr Turner hesitated. "He must have arrived after I left..."

Eliza's forehead creased. "He told us he was near your garden when Mr Hobson arrived. If you followed Mr Hobson..."

"No, it wasn't like that." Mr Turner rubbed a hand across his face. "As I told you, I watched Mr Hobson go into the maze, but about five minutes later, I saw Mr Swift go in after him. Knowing they were acquaintances, I presumed they'd planned a meeting and wanted to find out what they were talking about."

"And so you followed them?" Eliza glared at him. "That would mean you went to the maze *after* they arrived, not before?"

Mr Turner said nothing as he bowed his head.

Eliza sighed. "All right, so now we're getting somewhere. I'm guessing you went into the maze too."

"No." Mr Turner's head jerked up. "Or at least not far. I didn't go to the centre."

"Did you hear them talking together?"

Mr Turner fidgeted with his fingers. "Mr Swift said something about money, but I didn't hear much before footsteps came towards me and I panicked. That was when I hurried back to the garden."

"But you didn't bump into this person?"

"No, I was in one of the dead ends. Whoever it was must have known their way to the centre and missed me."

"Have you any idea whose footsteps they were?"

"No, I swear, I've no idea." Mr Turner pushed himself up from the table. "I'm sorry, it's time I was leaving."

"But you've not had dessert!" Connie's voice stopped Mr Turner, and he gazed at the apple pie on the sideboard.

"I don't think I could eat another thing. Thank you for the luncheon. It was very nice."

Eliza sat back in her chair as Archie escorted him to the door.

"Mr Turner."

He turned around to face her.

"Thank you. You've been a great help." She waited for

him to leave. "The problem is, he digs himself into a deeper hole every time we talk to him."

Henry chuckled. "I think you overwhelmed him."

"I don't know why. If he was telling the truth, it should have all been straightforward."

"So you think he's hiding something?" Connie asked.

"I don't know. I hope not, but he hasn't helped himself."

Archie rejoined them at the table. "At least he confirmed this Mr Swift is really Mr King."

"Yes, you're right. That was the main purpose of today, so we should be pleased. We must tell Inspector Adams in the morning. I expect he'll want to pay him a visit."

"Will we go too?" Connie asked.

"I hope so." Eliza grinned.

"The inspector won't want you with him if he's about to arrest him." Archie scowled. "This is police business now, Eliza. It's time you left them to it."

## CHAPTER SEVENTEEN

It had been a busy Monday morning, but as soon as the last person left the surgery, Eliza secured the lock on the door and hurried into the hall for her hat. The inspector should be in Moreton by now. If she was quick, she could nip to the station and be back by luncheon.

Sergeant Cooper was on the desk when she arrived, but his face fell as she walked in.

"Good morning, Mrs Thomson, are you on your own?"

"I'm afraid I am. I only want a quick word with the inspector, if he's here."

"Let me see if he's free." The sergeant disappeared into the back of the station but returned promptly with Inspector Adams.

"Mrs Thomson, I thought I recognised your voice. What can I do for you?"

Eliza smiled. "I've some news for you about Mr Swift."

"You do? Where did you get that from?"

Eliza's cheeks flushed. "From Mr Turner." She ignored the confusion on the inspector's face. "The thing is, as far as we know, he's the only person who saw Mr Swift at the palace and who had also seen him at the workshop with Mr Hobson. I wanted to check it was the same man, so I invited him to luncheon yesterday." She pursed her lips. "I also hoped he could confirm a hunch I had."

The inspector's eyes narrowed. "Go on."

"He did. We took a walk around the village after church and our Mr Swift appeared. Or should I say, Mr King."

"Mr Swift and Mr King are the same person?" Inspector Adams' mouth dropped open as Sergeant Cooper shook his head.

"Well I never!"

Eliza nodded. "Precisely. Mr Turner didn't even need prompting; as soon as Mr King stepped out of his front door, he recognised him."

Inspector Adams regained his composure. "Mrs Thomson, I'm sure I've a hundred questions about how you came to invite Mr Turner to Moreton, but for now I'll overlook them. I suppose we'd better pay Mr King a visit."

"That's why I called now. If you need to drive over to the bank in Kingston, I wanted to give you time to get the carriage ready. You'll also need time to work out what you'll ask him. I already have my own questions, so Mrs Appleton and I will be back here for one o'clock…"

"I hardly think that's necessary…"

"But you wouldn't have known anything about Mr King if it wasn't for me."

"And we're grateful, but we can take it from here."

"And what will you ask him?" Eliza's tone was harsher than she meant.

"We'll find out about his day at the palace, obviously, and find out why he was near the maze."

"Is that all?"

The inspector sighed. "All right, what have I missed?"

Eliza grinned. "If you let me come with you, I'll tell you."

"Mrs Thomson, this is no place for a…"

"Inspector, please don't say what I think you're going to say. You're well aware that I've helped with other cases."

The inspector threw up his hands. "Very well, but I can't allow you to sit in on the interview. Mr King's a respectable man. If there's a chance he's innocent…"

Eliza held up her hands. "I understand, but surely there'll be an anteroom where we can wait. If you leave the door ajar, we'll be able to hear…"

Inspector Adams shook his head. "Don't get carried away. I'll meet you back here at one. If you're late, we'll go without you!"

True to his word, as the church bells rang for one o'clock, Inspector Adams gave the signal for the carriage to pull away. Eliza sat opposite him, while Connie and Sergeant Cooper sat to her left. A quarter of an hour later, the carriage drove down the high street in Kingston-upon-Thames and came to a stop outside the bank.

Inspector Adams retrieved his hat as he climbed from the carriage. "Let me go in first and speak to Mr King. Sergeant Cooper, give me a couple of minutes and then escort the ladies inside; once they're settled, follow me into the office. I'll explain that we're waiting for you."

"Very good, sir." Sergeant Cooper remained seated and studied the second hand on his pocket watch for the full two minutes before helping Connie and Eliza onto the footpath. "Let me do the talking."

A clerk seated at a desk opposite the door looked up as they walked in, but scowled when he saw Eliza and Connie.

"Good afternoon, sir." Sergeant Cooper waited until he had the clerk's attention. "I'm here with Inspector Adams to see Mr King."

The clerk nodded. "Very good, sir ... but the ladies..."

"Ah, yes. I wonder if you have an outer office they can use while they wait. I'd rather not leave them outside, you see."

The clerk rose from his seat. "Of course, sir. I'll ask my colleague to join me out here and they can use his office."

"I'm much obliged." Sergeant Cooper followed the clerk into an anteroom and waited until Eliza and Connie were seated. Once they were settled, he was shown into the manager's office.

Eliza watched the clerk usher him inside, but groaned inwardly as he pulled the door closed behind him. Once he'd returned to his desk, she stood up to close the outer door behind him and tiptoed to Mr King's office.

"Let's find out where they're up to." She put an ear to the door to hear Inspector Adams talking.

"Let me remind you, sir, this is a murder investigation and as the last known person to see the victim alive, you're obliged to tell us what you know."

"I've told you, I don't know anything."

"Mr King, or should I say Mr Swift, we have witnesses who reported both you and Mr Hobson going into the maze shortly before his death. Now, unless you cooperate with this enquiry, you'll leave us with no choice but to take you to the station in Moreton for further questioning. So, will you tell us what you were doing and why you were using a false name?"

Mr King's impatience was clear. "All right, I admit I followed him into the maze, but I didn't kill him."

"So why did you do that?"

"He was a customer of the bank and I decided to speak to him about his investments."

"The maze seems a peculiar place for such a conversation."

"It was a spur-of-the-moment decision that seemed like a good idea at the time."

"So it wasn't prearranged?"

"No."

*Really?* Eliza raised an eyebrow at Connie and after a couple of seconds' silence, she bent down to peer through the keyhole.

"I happened to spot him in the grounds of the palace."

"That was convenient. Can you be more specific about where you were when you spotted Mr Hobson?"

"Now then, how can I describe it?" Mr King strolled to the window. "Ah, yes, I was by the tennis courts and he was walking along the path near the walled gardens."

The inspector sounded confused. "If I remember correctly, that's quite a distance. You must have excellent eyesight."

Mr King shrugged. "I suppose I do."

"And so you chased after him so you could speak to him about his investments?"

"No, not initially. I only wanted to wish him good day; that was all. I didn't want to appear rude."

"But I doubt he saw you if you were so far away."

Mr King gave a small cough. "No, well, maybe not, but I decided not to take any chances. If you must know, he was one of our wealthier clients and I was trying to be courteous."

Eliza caught the irritation in Inspector Adams' voice. "So, let me get this straight. You left your wife and children to chase after a wealthy customer, because of a slim chance you might hurt his feelings."

"Precisely. We like to take good care of our valued customers."

"And you expect us to ignore the fact that you followed him into the maze minutes before he was found dead?"

"Yes, because once I was inside, I got lost and couldn't find him. I wasn't in there long before I turned around and retraced my steps … thankfully." Mr King sounded slightly embarrassed. "I promise you, Inspector, it wasn't me who killed him. Why would I?"

"That, Mr King, is precisely what we're trying to determine. Can anyone confirm how long you were in the maze?"

"I couldn't say. My wife will tell you that I wasn't away from her for long. No more than five or ten minutes."

"But we understand you ran back to her across the grass; was that to give you an alibi?"

"I most certainly did not run on the grass; I wouldn't."

Eliza stared at the door. *But you were seen.*

Inspector Adams clearly thought the same. "We have a witness who saw you…"

"You may have, but they didn't see me on the grass." Mr King was most indignant and in the silence that followed, Eliza glimpsed the stand-off between the two men. It was Inspector Adams who spoke first.

"All right, it's not worth arguing about. Tell me instead why you'd visit Mr Hobson at his place of work in Molesey but use the name Swift."

Eliza could have sworn Mr King groaned.

"Listen, Inspector ... and Sergeant. It's not what it seems. Mr Hobson banked with us, but it was difficult for him to get to Kingston during working hours. It wasn't any trouble for me to go home via Molesey and so I offered to help out."

"So why would he set up a bank account in Kingston if he struggled to get here? Surely the branch in Molesey would be more convenient?"

"I really can't say ... you'd have to ask him."

"But we can't do that, can we, sir? Now, for the third time of asking, will you tell me why you used the name Swift instead of King?"

Mr King's shoulders sagged. "It's not exactly bank policy to visit clients, so I used an alias to keep a low profile. I didn't want other customers to expect a similar service."

"So why go to the workshop in the first place, if you were breaking bank protocol? As it is, using a false name makes you a prime suspect for his murder."

"But it's not like that ... I was trying to help."

"Because he was a wealthy client?"

"Yes. He gave us a lot of business and I wanted to keep him happy."

"Was that all it was, or was it because you wanted to keep him as a customer?" Inspector Adams walked towards the door then headed back to the desk. "Had Mr Hobson threatened to move his money to Molesey, on account of it being more convenient, and you were trying to stop him?"

When he was met with silence, Inspector Adams

continued. "I'll take that as a yes, which means the question is, would Mr Hobson moving his account be a motive for murder? Was his business worth so much?"

"No; not at all." Mr King's raised voice caused Eliza to flinch. "With Mr Hobson dead, the money will leave the bank, anyway. Why would I want that?"

"Where will it go?" Sergeant Cooper asked.

"I've no idea." Mr King was emphatic. "You'll need to speak to his solicitor."

"Can you tell us where we'll find him?"

"He didn't talk about such things. I'd suggest you try the practice in Molesey."

From the silence that followed, Sergeant Cooper's voice boomed into the room. "Will you excuse me for a moment? I've left something in the carriage." Eliza and Connie jumped back to their seats as the office door opened and Sergeant Cooper stepped out. The door shut behind him with a click as he leaned forward, his voice barely a whisper.

"What do you think? Is there anything else you'd like us to ask?"

Eliza pulled out her notebook and scribbled several questions onto a sheet of paper.

"First of all, we need to find out how he knew Mr Hobson was in the maze. We've two witnesses who said they arrived about five minutes apart. If that's the case, Mr King couldn't have seen Mr Hobson go in."

"That's a good point, that is." Sergeant Cooper stepped to the side to peer over Eliza's shoulder.

"Also, Mr Turner said he heard the two of them talking. How could that be if Mr King got lost?"

"Maybe there was someone else in there with them," Connie suggested.

"I suppose there could have been, but I'd expect Mr Turner to recognise the voices of Mr Hobson and Mr King, given he'd heard them both before. Let's ask Mr King anyway and see if he squirms."

Connie sighed. "I wish he would. He seems to have an answer to everything at the moment."

"It doesn't mean he's telling us the truth, though." Eliza paused. "You know, I'm also wondering where Mr Hobson got his money from. Father's already told us he had a history of larceny; did *all* his wealth come from illicit means?"

"Mr Turner seems to think so." Connie gazed at Sergeant Cooper as he blew out his cheeks.

"He must have had quite a racket going if it made him one of the bank's wealthiest clients."

"I'd say that's perfectly possible." Eliza stared up at the sergeant. "Perhaps you should find out when the account was set up. In fact, you should probably ask to see Mr Hobson's accounts; it may show us where the money came from and give us a clue as to who would want him dead."

Sergeant Cooper took the piece of paper from Eliza. "What if he won't tell us?"

"Remind him you're investigating a murder and the more he objects to sharing information, the more he makes himself appear guilty." She took the paper back from the sergeant and wrote a third question. "It might also be interesting to find out when he last visited Mr Hobson in Molesey."

Sergeant Cooper's brow creased. "Does it matter?"

Eliza cocked her head to one side. "That depends on the answer."

With the notes once again in his hand, Sergeant Cooper disappeared back into the office.

"Ah, Sergeant, you're here. Did you find what you were looking for?"

"Yes, sir. I'd left my notes in the carriage and I've realised there are a few more questions for Mr King."

Eliza smiled as she imagined the sergeant waving the paper in the air.

"So, what have we forgotten?"

There was such a pause that Eliza feared Sergeant Cooper was struggling with her handwriting. Finally, he cleared his throat.

"Right, so, Mr King said he followed Mr Hobson to the maze, but we have witnesses who say there was at least five minutes between them arriving. If that was the case, how did Mr King know Mr Hobson had actually gone into the maze?"

"I didn't, but I presumed he had. Where else would he be heading in that part of the garden?"

"He may have been going to the exit." Sergeant Cooper sounded pleased with himself. "I seem to remember the Lion Gate's in that vicinity."

"The palace had only just opened; why on earth would he be leaving?"

"He could have had his reasons." The sergeant's tone was defensive and Inspector Adams took over.

"But whether he did or not, you decided to go into the maze?"

"Yes, but when I couldn't find him, I left."

"That's interesting." Sergeant Cooper regained his stride. "We have a witness who overheard the two of you talking.

# THE PALACE MURDER

How do you explain that if you didn't meet with Mr Hobson?"

"I, erm ... I shouted to him. I've already told you, I got lost and panicked."

Inspector Adams couldn't keep the sarcasm from his voice. "You want us to believe that you had a conversation about his bank account by shouting through the hedges of the maze?"

"No, of course not. All I did was ask how he was, and..."

"And?"

"And if he needed any advice."

"And did he?"

"No. No, he didn't. He said everything was fine."

"Why on earth did you have a private conversation about his finances under such strange circumstances?" Inspector Adams' voice was raised. "Had you previously offered him advice, and he hadn't taken it?"

"It's standard practice for our priority customers."

"And did you ask him the same questions every time you saw him in the hope he'd give you more business?"

"Inspector Adams, I'm a bank manager and Mr Hobson was an important customer. I was only concerned for his best interests."

Eliza wouldn't have been surprised to hear Mr King stamp his foot, but Sergeant Cooper interrupted.

"Tell me, Mr King, when was the last time you visited Molesey?"

"When? I-I couldn't say, I don't keep a record. Maybe three or four weeks ago."

Inspector Adams continued. "So you saw him as recently as three weeks ago, and yet you shouted to him in a maze to ask if he needed advice? Forgive my cynicism, but something about all this doesn't ring true."

"Well it is, I promise."

"Or could it be that you were trying to get more business from him, but when he kept refusing, you lost your temper with him?"

"No, it was nothing like that. I swear he was still alive when I left the maze."

"How could you be so sure if you didn't see him?" Sergeant Cooper sounded triumphant.

"Because I heard him; I've already told you we spoke to each other through the hedge."

Eliza imagined Inspector Adams stepping between the two men as he spoke.

"All right, let's say you're telling the truth and Mr Hobson was alive when you left him. Were you aware of anyone else in the area?"

"No, I wasn't. I was frustrated at being lost and bothered about getting back to my wife. I wasn't paying attention to anything else."

"Very well, sir. May I ask one final question?" Sergeant Cooper paused. "You said that Mr Hobson was one of your wealthiest clients and yet he was only a foreman at a workshop that made railway parts. Do you know where his money came from?"

"I-I've no idea. It's not our business to ask such things."

"But it is ours. If you're not aware of where he got his money from, perhaps you could tell us how long Mr Hobson had banked with you. Had he already acquired the money by the time he moved back to Molesey?"

"Yes, I'm sure that's right. He's had his account here for years. Since before I started, I think."

"You think?"

Mr King gave an emphatic nod. "I'm positive."

"I'll have to ask you to show us all the details."

"S-show you what?"

Inspector Adams' voice rose above Sergeant Cooper's. "His bank account, sir. We need to see his bank account, right back to the day he opened it."

## CHAPTER EIGHTEEN

Eliza and Connie dashed back to their seats as the office door opened, but a second later they froze as Mr King stepped out and glared at them.

"You! What are you doing here? JOHNSON."

At the sound of his boss calling, the middle-aged man who had lent them his room came scurrying in.

"What's the meaning of this?"

"I'm sorry, sir. The officer asked if we could accommodate the ladies while they waited."

Mr King spun around to Sergeant Cooper. "You had no right to bring these women into my bank."

Sergeant Cooper pulled back his shoulders. "Don't you speak about Mrs Appleton like that. Or Mrs Thomson. They're fine ladies, they are."

"I don't care whether they are or not, they shouldn't be in my bank."

"I think you'll find we are allowed into banks." Eliza fixed her gaze on Mr King.

"And they're here at my request." Inspector Adams stepped forward. "Why are they causing you such concern?"

"Were they listening?" Mr King swivelled on the spot as five sets of eyes fixed on him. "They were, weren't they?"

"Maybe if you'd told us the truth that first evening we came to see you, it wouldn't have come to this." Eliza thought her heart would erupt from her chest as she fought to stay calm.

"I've nothing to hide, which you'll know if you've been listening. When I left the maze, Mr Hobson was alive and well."

"So you're upset because you don't want to share his bank account details." Eliza held his gaze. "Is that the problem?"

Mr King pulled on the edge of his jacket. "No, of course not. Why should that concern me?"

"Perhaps you could ask your clerk to fetch the relevant paperwork then." Inspector Adams raised his eyebrows as he indicated for Sergeant Cooper to escort Mr Johnson. "We don't want any papers to go missing, do we?"

Five minutes later, with three leather-bound ledgers lined up on the table in Mr King's office, Johnson left to return to his own desk. Eliza and Connie no longer bothered with the pretence of waiting for the police, and joined them to review the first ledger.

"Here we are. H to K. He'll be near the beginning of this section." Mr King turned the pages, his fingers trembling. "These are the records for 1895 to 1898, the time Mr Hobson joined our bank."

At the top of the third page was the name of Mr Gerard Hobson.

"Yes, here. He opened his account in September 1896

with quite an impressive sum. I believe that was when he moved back to Molesey."

"Five hundred pounds! Where on earth did a foreman get that sort of money?" Sergeant Cooper stared at the ledger.

"I really don't know." Mr King blanched as Inspector Adams glared at him.

"Could you tell us what trade Mr Hobson was in when he worked in London? Would it have attracted such an income?"

"I'm afraid I can't say. He was always rather secretive about his past. He liked to give the impression he was important, but I've no idea if he was." Mr King stepped forward to close the ledger, but Inspector Adams placed his hand on the page.

"Not yet, if you don't mind. Now, let's see what else is here." Inspector Adams ran a finger down the payments column.

"Nothing to suggest he paid in his weekly wage."

"Not unless he earned significantly more than everyone else at the workshop." Eliza pointed to several irregular amounts. "Look at these; one hundred pounds here, another for fifty pounds, one hundred and twenty-five."

"It looks to me as if it's the proceeds of the thefts." Sergeant Cooper rose up onto the balls of his feet. "Where else would he get that much money?"

Eliza studied Mr King. "Do you ever question unusually large payments?"

"Of course not. Client confidentiality is our duty. They should feel safe to use the bank for whatever they want."

"Even if they have a history of larceny?"

"Mr Hobson had no such thing." Mr King's left cheek

twitched. "To the best of my knowledge, he had no criminal record."

*Because he managed to talk his way out of it.* Eliza stepped across to the most recent ledger. "Shall we see if those payments continued?" She was about to open the book when Mr King blocked her. "Please, madam, this is no job for a lady. In fact, might I suggest you take a seat outside and I'll go through them with the inspector? You shouldn't be troubling yourself..."

"Trust me, Mr King, this is no trouble. Now, if you wouldn't mind turning to Mr Hobson's entries."

Reluctantly, Mr King found the Hs in the partially filled in ledger.

"Here we are." Eliza glanced at the inspector. "The payments continue, but are even higher."

"But have you noticed what's here?" Inspector Adams ran a finger down the expenses column. "Whenever a large amount of money was paid in, half of it was withdrawn within a week."

"Except for this last payment." Eliza tapped the page. "And there were smaller amounts drawn down at the same time. Mostly ten pounds. Can you tell us anything about those, Mr King?"

The bank manager took a step back. "Don't look at me. Maybe he wanted some living expenses; it's not uncommon."

"Drawing money out might not be, but taking out so much every couple of months strikes me as highly unusual. Especially when he received a wage. Have you any idea what he did with this cash?"

"No! I've not a clue."

"I wonder when this started." Eliza moved to the book

dated 1899 to 1902, and this time Mr King let her find the relevant page. "Here we are. The third week of January 1901, I would say. Were you at the bank by then, Mr King?"

Mr King nodded as he slipped further away from the table. "Yes, I was."

"When did you join?"

"The previous year. I don't recall when exactly."

"I do." All eyes turned to Connie, who looked at Eliza. "If you remember Mr and Mrs Wilson left Moreton in September 1900, and within a month or so, the house next door was sold to Mr King. If he started work at the bank around the same time as he moved to Moreton, it must have been October or November 1900."

Eliza beamed at her friend. "You're right! Well remembered. Was that the case, Mr King?"

"Erm ... yes, it sounds plausible."

Eliza raised an eyebrow to Connie and returned her attention to the ledger. "So that means the withdrawals from the account started within a couple of months of you becoming manager."

Mr King shrugged. "I fail to see the significance of that statement."

Eliza stared at him. *Yes, unfortunately so do I, but I don't believe it's a coincidence.* "Very well." She turned to the inspector. "Let me make a note of these figures and then we need to find the solicitor. If there's a will with a beneficiary we haven't come across yet, we'll need to speak to them."

"You can't do that. Those records are confidential." Mr King's voice squeaked once more.

"And this is a murder investigation, Mr King." Inspector Adams waited for Eliza to take the notebook from her handbag before he read out details of the payments and withdrawals. It took over five minutes for him to reach the last entry. "There, that should do it."

"Splendid." Eliza tucked the notes back into her bag. "Did you make a copy too, Sergeant?"

"I did indeed. We won't always be travelling together."

"No, quite." Inspector Adams reached for his hat. "We'll leave it at that for now, Mr King. Thank you for your time."

"Oh, one more question." Eliza's voice stopped the inspector where he was.

"Go on."

"We didn't ask about a will." She glanced over to Mr King. "Before we go in search of a solicitor, do you know if he made one?"

"As I said, I've no idea, we didn't discuss it, although I'd be surprised if he hadn't."

Eliza cocked her head to one side. "Really? Why?"

"Mr Hobson lived on his own and had no children. As far as I'm aware, the only living relative he had was a brother and he wouldn't want anything going to him."

"The brother!" Eliza's eyes were wide as she gaped at Inspector Adams. "Why wouldn't he want his money to pass to him?"

Mr King shrugged. "I don't know the details other than the fact he hated him."

"You're not the first person to say that. Do you have any idea why?"

Mr King's voice was once again steady. "No, not directly. The only thing I can tell you is that until recently, the brother lived with their mother. When she died, Mr Hobson saw him at the funeral, but he commented afterwards that he was glad his brother's father was already dead, otherwise he wouldn't have attended."

Eliza gaped at Mr King. "His brother's father?"

"That's what he said."

"Not *his* father?" Excitement coursed through her as Mr King shook his head and she spun around to Inspector Adams. "If they had different fathers, Mr Hobson and his brother would have different surnames. That would explain why you can't find a second Mr Hobson!" Without waiting for a response, she spun back to Mr King. "You don't happen to have the brother's name, do you?"

"No, I'm sorry, it was never mentioned. It was always 'that brother of mine'. I do know he was younger than Mr Hobson though, because Mr Hobson's mother was widowed and then remarried."

"That's most helpful. Thank you, Mr King."

Eliza waited until the carriage had moved away from the footpath before she spoke. "That was interesting."

"It most certainly was." Inspector Adams smiled at her. "Well done for asking about the will. I'd completely forgotten about it with everything else going on."

"I nearly had myself. I still think Mr King's hiding something, though. I just can't work out what it is."

"I spotted that." Connie settled her handbag on her knee. "When he was telling us about the brother, his tone was perfectly normal, but if you asked him anything about the money, he was much more uncomfortable."

Eliza grinned. "That's exactly it! I'm sure he knows something about the withdrawals, but being able to prove it is another matter."

Inspector Adams had sat quietly stroking his moustache.

"I think we need to find out where the money came from first and see if it actually was stolen. It was good thinking to write the amounts down."

"Do you think Mr King knows whether Mr Hobson stole it?" Connie asked.

Eliza gazed out of the window. "It really wouldn't surprise me. I also had the rather outlandish idea that Mr King had known about it and threatened to report Mr Hobson to the police unless he shared the money with him."

"Which would explain why half of it was drawn out again?" Inspector Adams clicked his tongue, but Sergeant Cooper's brow furrowed.

"Why would he do that, though? Wouldn't it have been easier and less obvious if Mr Hobson had just handed it to Mr King, without paying it into his account?"

"Only if it was cash." Eliza frowned as thoughts raced through her mind. "If they used cheques, it would have required two transactions."

The inspector spoke slowly. "Which would explain Mr King's visits to the workshop."

"It would indeed." Eliza saw Connie and Sergeant Cooper exchanging glances. "Don't worry. I'll explain later."

## CHAPTER NINETEEN

Eliza stood up from the breakfast table and reached for her handbag as Archie watched her.

"I'm sorry to leave you like this, but you understand, don't you?"

"Would it matter if I didn't?"

"Of course it would, but it's taken me over a week to get Inspector Adams to take me and Connie to Molesey, I could hardly turn him down when he invited us."

"Well, try not to be all day. You need to make up the prescriptions this afternoon."

"I will, but you needn't wait to have luncheon if we're not back in time. I've asked Cook to put something to one side for us." With her coat over her arm, she hurried through the front door before Archie changed his mind.

Connie was waiting by her garden gate when Eliza emerged from the house. "Here you are. I was about to come and see where you were."

"It's all right, we've a couple of minutes yet. Now, let me check I've got everything." She rummaged in her bag. "Yes, the notebook is there, I don't want to go without that. In fact, I need to sit down later and read through it to make sure I've not missed anything."

Connie nudged her. "Well, you've no time now, the carriage is here."

Sergeant Cooper climbed down to greet them as soon as the driver opened the door for him. "Good morning, ladies. Another lovely day."

Connie's cheeks flushed as the sergeant extended his hand to her. "Good morning, Sergeant."

Eliza climbed the steps unaided. "Good morning, Inspector."

"Mrs Thomson." He partially rose from his seat. "Let's hope it turns out to be."

"Indeed." She waited until Sergeant Cooper had taken his seat. "Where will we go first, the solicitors or workshop?"

"The solicitors, I think. It could take half the morning to find out which one he used, and we need to know who benefits from the will. Once we find that out, the men in the workshop may be able to tell us more."

"I suppose it could even be someone from the workshop."

Inspector Adams gave a wry smile. "Wouldn't that be nice?"

The journey to Molesey was uneventful and as they reached the bridge to cross the river, they took a left-hand turn into the village.

"I asked the coachman to drive slowly down the main street so we can look out for all the solicitors' offices." Inspector Adams gazed out of the window. "I didn't have time to contact anyone for details."

"That was a good idea. I'd rather not walk all the way

back down here, if we don't need to." Eliza stared out of the same window as the inspector, while Connie and Sergeant Cooper peered through the other.

"There's one, and another." Sergeant Cooper's pencil scratched on the paper of his notepad.

"There's one on this side too." Inspector Adams groaned. "This could be a long morning."

By the time the carriage reached the far end of the village, they'd counted five solicitors' offices.

"Shall we split up?" Sergeant Cooper asked. "It would save a bit of shoe leather."

Inspector Adams nodded. "It would save time too. Mrs Thomson, you go with Sergeant Cooper, I'll take Mrs Appleton."

Eliza didn't miss the pout on the sergeant's face, but Inspector Adams appeared not to notice.

"Sergeant, if you find the solicitor's in question, come back outside and wait for me. I want to ask the questions. Is that clear?"

"Yes, sir."

"Would it be possible for me to be there too?" Eliza gave the inspector one of her best smiles.

A resigned look crossed his face. "All right, I'll stand outside for you, but you'll need to keep your wits about you. I don't want to spend the morning hanging around. Thankfully, the offices are all close together."

As they split up, Sergeant Cooper led Eliza towards the first office on the right-hand side of the street.

"Here we are." He peered through the window. "You can't see much through there. Come on, let's find out what they know."

A young clerk jumped up from a desk near the door as soon as he saw Sergeant Cooper's uniform.

"Officer. What can I do for you?"

"It's all right, laddie. No need to worry. I'm investigating the death of a Mr Gerard Hobson and would like to know if your practice represented him."

The clerk eyed Sergeant Cooper as he gave him a wide berth. "Let me check the files. The name doesn't sound familiar."

Eliza watched as the young man flicked through the papers in a drawer, slowly at first and then with more urgency.

"No, I'm sorry, we don't seem to have him as a client. Have you tried next door?"

"Not yet, but we will. Thank you."

As they left the office, Eliza studied the opposite side of the road in search of Inspector Adams. "They don't appear to be having any more success than us."

"It's still early days. Let's keep going." Sergeant Cooper led the way to their next stop, and after holding open the door for Eliza, he repeated his prepared speech to an equally young clerk. Once again after much searching through their records, the answer was the same.

"You could try next door."

"I'm afraid we have and they couldn't help either."

The clerk's face dropped but quickly brightened. "What about over the road?"

"My colleague, Inspector Adams, is already there."

"Oh." This time the smile was slower to return. "I've an idea. If you turn right out of here and take the first right again, there's another office down there. It's only a small place, but they may have what you're looking for."

Sergeant Cooper beamed to the clerk. "Thank you, laddie, you've been very helpful."

As soon as they were outside, Eliza again scanned the street for Inspector Adams and Connie. "There they are. They must have called at all three of their offices."

"It wouldn't surprise me, that second place we visited took their time."

Eliza smiled as the inspector joined them. "Have you had any joy?"

"No, I'm afraid not. I presume you've not either."

Sergeant Cooper answered. "No, sir, but we've one more office to try."

"You've only visited one?"

"No, sir, we've done the two on this side, but apparently there's another place down a side street on the right. Shall I lead the way?"

"Please do." Inspector Adams joined Sergeant Cooper as they disappeared down the side street. Eliza and Connie followed them only to find Sergeant Cooper standing outside a dingy-looking office.

"Is this it?" Eliza gaped at it. "Is it even open?"

"It says M. D. Jones, Solicitor on the plaque, so let's see." Inspector Adams stepped forward and clicked on the latch before pushing open the door. "So far, so good."

The front room was empty except for a wooden table and four chairs, which were covered in a layer of dust.

Connie tutted. "You'd think they'd make more of an effort."

"Who's there?"

Eliza and Connie moved closer together as a voice called from beyond an archway in the back corner.

"Inspector Adams from New Scotland Yard and Sergeant Cooper. May we come through?"

Without giving an answer, an elderly man with an ill-fitting suit and a thin layer of grey hair strolled into the room.

"What do you want?"

"We're looking for Mr Jones, the solicitor."

"Why?"

"We'd like to ask him a few questions about a possible client."

"He ain't got none."

Inspector Adams exchanged a glance with Eliza. "No clients? But the sign outside…"

"He only had one and the fool's gone and got himself killed."

Eliza couldn't contain her curiosity. "This client wouldn't have been a Mr Gerard Hobson, would it?"

The man's watery eyes swivelled in her direction as if he'd only just noticed her. "What is it to you?"

"Please, sir, if you'd answer the question?" Inspector Adams didn't take his eyes from the man.

"What if it was? He's dead now."

"But his solicitor works here? May we speak with him?"

The man continued to stare until he muttered something to himself and turned to leave the room. "Stay here."

Eliza held her breath as they waited for him to return, but was surprised to hear somewhat heavier footsteps approaching. Moments later, a tall, well-dressed man appeared.

"Gentlemen." He gave the officers a slight bow. "Father says you'd like a word. How may I help?"

Sergeant Cooper took out his notepad. "Are you Mr Jones, the solicitor mentioned on the plaque outside?"

"Yes, sir, I am."

Inspector Adams offered him a hand. "We're here about a Mr Gerard Hobson and we understand you work on his behalf."

"I used to."

"So you'll be aware he was murdered recently? We need to know if he left a last will and testament."

Mr Jones kept up his professional demeanour, but his jaw clenched. "He died without making one."

Eliza's forehead furrowed as Inspector Adams asked the question she was thinking.

"He died without a will? A man with so much money?"

"I'm afraid I wasn't privy to how much his personal property amounted to. All I can say is that he had recently instructed me to prepare a will on his behalf, but we hadn't got around to detailing his assets."

"Did he tell you who the beneficiaries of the estate would be?"

"No. As I say, we were at an early stage."

Eliza watched Mr Jones as the silence mounted. "Forgive me for asking, but we've heard that Mr Hobson had a brother. Are you aware of him?"

Mr Jones gave a sarcastic laugh. "Oh, yes indeed, I even saw him several weeks ago outside this office. Not that we were introduced. Mr Hobson was furious about him being here and they had quite an argument. Apparently, he disliked his brother so much, he made a point of telling him that I was in the process of preparing his last will and testament. Not that I was, but he wanted his brother to be sure he'd receive nothing. As soon as his brother disappeared, he told me to start working on it."

"But without a will, the brother must stand to inherit his estate? Assuming there were no children or other siblings." Eliza stared at Inspector Adams. "That's got to be a motive for murder."

The inspector nodded. "And a good one at that. Could you tell us the brother's name, Mr Jones? We've heard the two men were only half-brothers and so had different surnames."

Mr Jones shook his head. "He divulged very little information to me. The only reason he kept me on was so I could provide a defence for him as and when he found himself in trouble."

Eliza's head jerked up from her notepad. "You mean the larceny?"

"Yes, I do. He always claimed his innocence, but I've never defended anyone who was accused of as many misdemeanours as him."

"But you were the one who saved him from the cells?"

"I was, although a fat lot of good it did me." He glanced around at the shoddy surroundings. "Ten pounds a month to retain my services didn't last long."

*That explains that then.* "Was Mr Hobson your only client?"

Mr Jones paced the floor. "Unfortunately, he was. For years, he'd promised he'd reward my loyalty on condition that I only worked for him. At one point, he promised to shower me with riches, but then we had a particularly difficult defence and his enthusiasm waned. By the end, he owed me rather a lot of money."

Eliza cocked her head to one side. "This difficult defence wouldn't have been when he left London, would it?"

Mr Jones spun around to face her. "It was. He worked for a company in Whitechapel who accused him of stealing over two hundred pounds. They had a witness who testified that they saw him altering some ledgers, and he spent time in the cells while we mounted his defence. He wasn't happy about that."

"But you had him freed?"

"I did, but it was touch and go." Mr Jones sighed.

"But he didn't sack you?"

"No, interestingly he didn't; he said he wanted me available in case I was needed again. The thing is, I've had a lot of time to think since then, and I decided I probably knew too much. If he'd fired me when he was released, I could have made life difficult for him. I suppose he realised that."

"So you think he was guilty?"

"With the benefit of hindsight, I'm afraid I do."

Sergeant Cooper glared at the solicitor. "Why didn't you report him then? That makes you as bad as him."

"Perhaps." Mr Jones shrugged. "I did try to talk to him about it, but every time I did, he convinced me I was right to defend him."

Inspector Adams studied Mr Jones. "We suspect Mr Hobson was paying someone to cover up his crimes. Is that how he persuaded you to stay quiet?"

"Really, Inspector, does it look as if I've got money to spare?" Mr Jones waved an arm around the unkempt office. "As I've said, he owed me a lot of money."

"Looks can be deceptive, sir, and that is a rather smart suit you're wearing."

Mr Jones laughed. "My appearance is everything, Inspector; it's all I spend my money on. If I don't dress smartly, I've no chance of finding new clients."

"Cleaning the office might help." Connie put a hand to her mouth as she realised she'd spoken out loud.

Mr Jones straightened his back. "And I'll do that if I'm able to make a claim against Mr Hobson's estate for unpaid work."

Inspector Adams hadn't taken his eyes off Mr Jones. "I'm not sure that I believe all this pleading poverty. I need you to show us your bank statements ... back to January 1901."

Mr Jones glared at the inspector. "Are you accusing me of being in collusion with Mr Hobson? I'd suggest you retract that statement immediately if you don't want me to sue you for slander."

"I'm not accusing you, sir, but I'd like to rule it out of our enquiries. Now, if you wouldn't mind."

Eliza and Connie stayed where they were as the police officers followed Mr Jones into his office.

"What do you think?" Connie whispered.

"I'm not certain, but I'd say he's telling the truth. If he'd been given the sums of money we saw in the bank ledgers, he wouldn't leave the office like this."

"That's what I thought. If Mr Hobson always gave the appearance of having money, you'd expect his solicitor to do the same if he was being paid handsomely."

Eliza paced the room once more. "And this amount of dust hasn't accumulated since a week last Saturday. It's taken months to get this thick."

"You mean if he wanted to set himself up to have an alibi?"

"Yes, exactly. The thing is, I suspect the large withdrawals from Mr Hobson's account were to pay someone to keep quiet."

Eliza's thoughts were disturbed by the three gentlemen returning.

"Everything appears above board." Inspector Adams was less than pleased as he walked past the ladies. "It's time we went to the workshop to find out what Mr Hobson's workmates can tell us."

## CHAPTER TWENTY

The carriage had followed them up the high street, and Inspector Adams helped the ladies aboard for their short journey to the workshop.

"I presume there were no unusual payments to Mr Jones' bank account." Eliza straightened her skirt as the horses pulled away.

"Not a one." The frustration in the inspector's voice was noticeable. "In fact, he received nothing except for the monthly ten pounds."

"His fee for acting as Mr Hobson's defence in court?"

"Exactly." The inspector banged a hand on his knee. "I was sure he had to be involved."

"Perhaps Mr Hobson paid him in cash and he never paid it into his account." Connie's eyes flitted between Eliza and the inspector.

The inspector considered it. "Maybe. It's a lot to keep as cash, though."

"It is." Eliza nodded. "But don't be too despondent; I'm sure you're on the right lines. The more I think about it, the more I'm convinced Mr Hobson used those large sums of money to keep someone quiet."

"You're probably right. The question is, how do we prove it, and would that same person want him dead?"

"I'm not sure it makes sense for the person who was blackmailing him to be our murderer." Eliza sighed. "If he *was* being blackmailed, it would make more sense if Mr Hobson was the killer."

"To stop the payments being necessary, you mean?" Connie stared at her.

"Exactly."

"In that case, I'd expect to see signs of a scuffle." Sergeant Cooper put his hands on his hips. "But we didn't."

"No, we didn't." Inspector Adams blew out through his lips. "We need to give this some more thought."

The carriage drew to a halt, and the coachman helped them down the steps before Inspector Adams led the way into the workshop. A burly-looking man wearing overalls, and with soot on his face, wandered over to them.

"You were here the other day, weren't you?"

Inspector Adams nodded. "We're here to see Mr Coates. Is he in?"

"This way." The man showed them to a door and, following one knock, pushed it open. "The bobbies are back."

Mr Coates jumped to his feet as Inspector Adams strode into the room and extended his hand.

"Good morning, Mr Coates. You remember me. This is Sergeant Cooper and these ladies are accompanying us."

Mr Coates studied Eliza and Connie as he gestured for the inspector to take a seat.

"What can I do for you?"

"We're here about Mr Hobson again, but this time, I'd like to ask whether you've suffered any thefts over the last few years."

"You mean men thieving stock?"

"Possibly, although I was thinking more about money."

"Money? No. Not since we had that problem with Mr Turner, anyway."

Eliza watched Inspector Adams' shoulders slump and stepped forward. "Do you mind me asking whether you do your own accounts?"

"Not me personally. I've several clerks and Mr Hobson would help…"

Eliza glared at Mr Coates. "Mr Hobson did the accounts?"

Inspector Adams' face coloured. "I understood Mr Hobson was a foreman, not a clerk."

"He was. He didn't actually do the bookkeeping, he'd just help out with the entries at the end of each day. One of the clerks would do all the totting up. They've struggled since the business expanded, and rather than hiring someone else, Mr Hobson offered to help. He was so generous with his time."

"We'll need to see your accounts." Inspector Adams scratched his head. "I'm sorry to tell you, but we've reason to believe Mr Hobson was taking substantial amounts of money from the business."

Mr Coates' mouth fell open. "Mr Hobson? No, you've got that wrong."

"It's possible we have, but we really do need to check your books. If you wouldn't mind."

With a moment's hesitation, Mr Coates stood up and led Inspector Adams into an adjacent office. Eliza made sure she and Connie were right behind Sergeant Cooper as he stepped into a poorly lit office where four clerks sat, each hunched over a ledger.

Mr Coates clapped his hands together. "Gentlemen, may I have your attention? This is Inspector Adams, and he needs to check our records back to 1901. Would you indulge him?"

With a degree of muttering, the clerks stood up and retrieved a selection of leather-bound books from the shelves. Inspector Adams surveyed them on the large wooden table where they'd placed them. "Where do we start?"

Eliza eyed the ledgers. "Could you tell us which records relate to the purchase of materials?"

The eldest of the men stepped forward, his rounded shoulders suggesting he'd been bent over these documents for most of his life. "Here you are." He opened the book in the centre of the table. "We've been busy these last few years. We're getting through more parts than ever."

Eliza and Inspector Adams stood in front of the documents, staring at the rows and rows of numbers on the page.

The inspector drummed his fingers on the desk. "This could take forever."

"It could, but may I check something?" Eliza reached into her bag for her notebook. "May we see the entries for January?"

Inspector Adams turned the pages until he reached the start of the year. "What are we looking for?"

Eliza reread her notes. "The fifth of January. Was there a payment made of eighty-five pounds, three shilling and fourpence?"

The inspector ran his finger down the dates until he

arrived at the fifth and moved it across the expenses. "Yes, here. There were several payments that day, but there was one for that exact amount to GH Manufactory."

Eliza examined the entry before turning back to her notes. "What about on the twentieth? Was there anything to GH Manufactory?"

"There was, for one hundred and five pounds, dead."

Eliza stared at the ledger. "Look, there are another three payments to the same place." She flicked forward to February. "There are more here. I'd be surprised if they don't correspond to the amounts and dates I got from the bank."

Inspector Adams turned back to the clerk. "Were all these transactions checked against the invoices?"

"Yes, sir. I will have done most of them myself, but Mr Hobson would often help us out, so he may have done some."

"GH." Eliza tapped her finger on the ledger. "Could it stand for Gerard Hobson?"

"I would say it's highly likely." His eyes didn't leave the clerk. "Do you have the invoices for these payments?"

"I'm sure we will have; let me fetch them for you."

The man scurried to a bank of drawers on the far side of the room and lifted out a wad of papers. "This is everything we have for that month." He banged them down on the table. "Now, let me see. What dates are we looking for?"

He flicked through the pile until he came to the fifth of January. "GH Manufactory?" He scanned each document twice. "We don't seem to have that one."

"What about the twentieth?"

The clerk shook his head. "No."

The inspector sucked air through his teeth. "So, he was taking money from the company without anyone realising it."

The colour disappeared from the clerk's face. "We never enter anything without an invoice. I always check…"

"Unless Mr Hobson told you he'd already done it?"

The clerk put a hand to his head. "I'm so sorry, Mr Coates."

"Oh my goodness, I've had a thought." Eliza suddenly flicked through the pages. "Here we are, September 1902." She studied the page. "There's no mention of a GH Manufactory, but see here, a payment to Turner & Sons for four hundred and six pounds. That was the figure quoted in the newspaper for Mr Turner's trial." Eliza stared up at the clerk, who looked close to collapse. "Is there an invoice for that?"

"There should have been one for the trial." Inspector Adams helped himself to the paperwork, but Mr Coates stopped him.

"I'm afraid you're wasting your time. There is no invoice. That was the whole basis for the prosecution, that Mr Turner had allocated the money to himself, but we had no invoice to show what it was for."

"But he was found to be innocent?"

Mr Coates nodded. "Because there was no evidence he had the money."

Eliza ran her fingers over the ledger. "So, it's as if Mr Hobson deliberately used Mr Turner's name to make him look guilty."

The inspector scowled at the clerk. "Did Mr Turner ever help with the accounts when he worked here?"

"Not that we know, sir, but on the day of that entry, we were aware that someone had tampered with the books. We always stack them neatly at night, but they were all open the following morning when we came in."

"So you think the person who filled in that transaction wanted it to be discovered?" Eliza studied Mr Coates, who was almost as pale as the clerk.

"It was Mr Hobson who found it. I remember it vividly because he came to tell me about it and was furious that anyone would do such a thing to the company."

"And it was him who pressed for the prosecution? What did Mr Turner say about it?"

"He denied it, naturally, and I must admit, I was of a mind to believe him, but Mr Hobson wouldn't let it drop. He reported it to the police and pushed them to take it to trial, even though there was no evidence that Mr Turner had the money."

"And you let him?" Eliza gasped.

"He said he was doing it for me. He could be very persuasive when he wanted to be."

"But once they'd found Mr Turner not guilty, you didn't pursue charges on anyone else."

"Oh no, we'd had quite enough; and the legal bills were too high as it was."

Eliza's eyes narrowed. "Who did you use as your solicitor?"

"Oh, now you're asking. Let me think … Mr Hobson dealt with all that."

"Could it have been a Mr Jones?"

"Yes, that was it." Mr Coates pointed a finger at Eliza. "Not that I met him; Mr Hobson represented the company."

"And you paid the solicitor for the work he did?"

"Yes, of course. I'm a man of my word. Over one hundred pounds it cost me."

Eliza reached once more for her notebook. "Do you remember when you paid this money?"

Mr Coates scratched his head. "It was as instalments of about twenty pounds a week. The details should be in here." He flicked through the ledger until he found the entries he was after. "Here you are. They started before the trial in December and then ended in January. All duly noted as being paid to Mr Jones."

Eliza and the inspector exchanged glances before Inspector Adams focused again on Mr Coates.

"There was no mention of any payments into Mr Jones' account. How did you pay him? With a cheque?"

"Oh no. We always have cash in the safe and so I'd give it to Mr Hobson to take to Mr Jones."

Eliza's heart sank, and she took a deep breath as she consulted her notebook. "I'm afraid that money didn't reach Mr Jones." She showed her notes to Inspector Adams and Mr Coates. "The dates here, from Mr Hobson's bank records, show that he paid himself twenty pounds the day after each of those withdrawals noted in your ledger."

The inspector peered over Eliza's shoulder. "And Mr Jones told us that Mr Hobson owed him rather a lot of money."

"What a horrible man he must have been." Connie's voice felt like a breath of fresh air in what had become an uncomfortably warm office.

Mr Coates ran a hand over his face. "The thing is, he wasn't. He was always very agreeable; the perfect employee to be honest, always did his best for the business."

"Except he was fooling you." Eliza stabbed a finger at the ledger. "I'd suggest we check these figures alongside Mr Hobson's accounts. It won't take long if we take them to Moreton with us."

"It might give Mr Jones the evidence he needs to make a claim against the estate too."

The sun was bright as they stepped outside, and Eliza squinted as her eyes adjusted to the light.

"I don't know how they work in that office day after day. They mustn't see daylight in the winter."

"It's one of the reasons I applied for a job with the police." Sergeant Cooper moved to one side as Eliza and Connie climbed into the carriage. "I couldn't do with being cooped up like that."

"They get well paid for it though." Inspector Adams took the ledgers from the sergeant. "Not that I'd swap. Now, what are we going to do with these?"

"If you let me have them, I'll go through them later." Eliza looked at Connie. "You'll come around and help, won't you?"

"Of course I will. They'll be so much easier to read on the desk in the dispensary."

Inspector Adams nodded. "Very well. Sergeant Cooper and I have a few other things to attend to this afternoon, so shall we call at the surgery at about four o'clock to see if you've found anything?"

Eliza searched for a clock, but didn't find one. "What time is it?"

"A quarter to twelve."

"By the time we get home and have luncheon, that won't give us much time. *Not to mention the prescriptions I'll have waiting for me.* Could you come a little later, say half past six, once we've had dinner?"

The church bells had rung out for two o'clock when Connie joined Eliza in the dispensary.

"How are you getting on?"

"Slowly! I think Archie deliberately prescribed ointments that need preparing from scratch. I'm not even halfway through. Would you like to help? I daren't start the accounts until these are done."

"I don't know how I can." Connie gaped at the bottles on the counter.

"Don't worry, I won't ask you to make anything. If you could just put things into these bottles and add a label, that would be a great help."

The two of them worked quietly for the next hour, until finally, at three o'clock, Eliza fastened the lid on the last jar. "I'd say that calls for a cup of tea. She rang a small handbell on the counter. I think we'd better take it in here, don't you?"

"As long as we can sit down. My feet are tired from all the walking we did, not to mention the standing up."

Eliza chuckled. "We can manage that. I can't wait to go through these ledgers, though. I've a feeling we're going to find something of interest."

By the time the tea arrived, Eliza had the books laid out on the wooden table in the middle of the room, their pages opened to the first week of January 1901. She waited for the maid to leave before she turned her attention to them.

"Right, this is where Mr Hobson started making large payments into his account. Shall we check for entries paid to GH Manufactory first?"

Connie ran a finger down the list of creditors. "Nothing on this page."

Eliza opened her notebook. "Let me see when the first payment was made. Here we are, the twentieth of January for twenty pounds, three shillings and sixpence. What's in the ledger?"

Connie put a finger under the corresponding amount withdrawn from Mr Coates' account the day prior to the payment. "What does that say? Locks?"

"Yes, I would say so, although the handwriting's particularly bad. Are there any more payments to them?"

Connie flipped over the page. "Not by the end of March. Do you have any more dates?"

"The next one is on the fifth of February for thirty-nine pounds, six shillings."

Connie again found the entry. "Here we are. Recorded as being paid to Saviles. I think. The handwriting is difficult for this too."

Eliza continued to work her way through the expenses. "Here, as well; Lobbs. Are you noticing a pattern here?"

"Saviles, Locks and Lobbs." Connie's brow was furrowed. "All very fancy men's outfitters."

"Exactly. That would explain why he was so smartly dressed."

Connie gasped. "And Mr Coates was paying the bills."

"And more besides, I would say. He couldn't possibly spend that much money on hats and shoes."

They continued to scan the ledger, searching for similar patterns.

"He certainly knew how to treat himself. Look at these stores. Harrods, Fenwick's..." Connie put a hand to her chest.

"My goodness."

"I don't suppose he paid them everything he drew out, though. It's as if he used the names as a reference."

"So when did he start using GH Manufactory instead?" Eliza leafed through several pages before she reached November 1902. "Here, shortly after he accused Mr Turner of larceny."

"I wonder why he changed."

Eliza shrugged. "Maybe he was running out of names to use. I think he'd already referenced every reputable supplier in London."

"Or it could have been to make it appear more professional." Connie studied Eliza. "Perhaps it was becoming obvious that he was referencing stores, but by calling himself a manufactory, it would give the impression of the payment being to a legitimate business."

"That's an excellent point. We should probably check with Mr Jones how many times he needed to defend him once he changed the way he operated. In fact..." Eliza turned to 1901 "...let's make a note of all the suppliers he claimed to have paid while we've got the chance. You never know when these things might come in handy."

They worked diligently for the next half hour, Connie reading out the details and Eliza writing them all down. As she reached August 1902, Connie let out a gasp.

"Oh goodness, look at this."

Eliza finished her note before she glanced up. "What is it?"

"The entry for the fifteenth of August."

"King. King!" Eliza's eyes widened. "I knew he was involved. How much was it for?"

"Ninety-seven pounds, twelve shillings and tenpence."

Eliza stood up to pace the room. "Right, let's stay calm. This doesn't mean Mr King knew anything about this. Mr Hobson could have used his name as a reference, as he did with the shops."

"But if we suspect he used the shop names because he did actually owe them money, then the same might be true here. He may not have paid Mr King the full ninety-seven pounds, but he may have given him part of it."

"Yes, you're right. You know what this means, don't you? We need to ask Inspector Adams to check Mr King's bank records. Let's see if any of Mr Hobson's withdrawals correspond to money paid into his accounts."

Connie shuddered. "He won't like that."

"No, he won't, and for once I might suggest Inspector Adams and Sergeant Cooper go without us."

## CHAPTER TWENTY-ONE

With surgery over for another day, Eliza stood in the dispensary window staring out across the green. Over the course of the morning, she'd tried her best to keep an eye out for passing traffic, but either Inspector Adams wasn't back from Kingston, or she hadn't seen him arrive.

She sighed as the gong sounded for luncheon. She didn't think she'd missed him; besides, Connie would have called if she'd spotted him, but there'd been no sign of her either.

Once she got to the dining room, she found Mr Bell on his own. He looked up as she approached the table.

"You seem very subdued."

"I'm just wondering how Inspector Adams is getting on with Mr King. I expected him to be back by now." Eliza smiled at Archie as he and Henry joined them.

"It will take a while if they need to go through all Mr King's accounts."

"Surely not that long, though."

"It would if Mr King denies everything and refuses to

answer their questions." Henry took a seat next to his mother. "We know he has quite a temper."

Eliza nodded. "We do, but I doubt Inspector Adams would stand for him causing any trouble. I'll call at the police station later in case I've missed them."

"Don't you think you've helped enough already?" Archie gave her an affectionate smile. "You should let them finish the job themselves."

"If Mr King's our murderer then I will, but there's still a chance he isn't. I suspect he was involved with the larceny or fraud, but I'm not convinced about the murder." Eliza sliced into the piece of liver that sat beside some mashed potatoes.

"It wouldn't surprise me, he's a strange man." Archie focused on his food, but Eliza stopped to study him.

"Do you remember the day we visited the palace, you said it surprised you to see him on the trip with the family. Why did you say that?"

Archie shrugged. "He's never struck me as a sociable chap. I've only been to the house on a couple of home visits, but on both occasions he was rather unpleasant. Not to mention a bully to his wife. I didn't expect a church day out to be his idea of relaxation."

Eliza put down her knife and fork. "Do you think he arranged the meeting with Mr Hobson and took the family along to act as an alibi?"

Archie sat back, a smirk appearing on his face. "Under normal circumstances, I'd say you were being ridiculous, but as it is, you could be right."

Eliza beamed at him. "Really! I need to speak to Inspector Adams as soon as possible. I don't want Mr King disappearing because they let him off the hook."

Eliza didn't bother finishing her cup of tea before she fixed her hat and headed next door to Connie's. She knocked and walked straight in.

"Have you finished luncheon?"

Connie appeared from the scullery in the far corner of the room. "Yes, I'm just washing up, why? Is Inspector Adams back?"

"That's what we need to find out; get your coat on."

They took the quickest way to the station and once they were past the shop and church, they rounded the bend to see the blue glass lantern on the front of the building. The police carriage, with the horses standing patiently in front of it, waited outside. Eliza shook her head.

"How did we both manage to miss them? Look, they're here."

Constable Jenkins was on the desk as Eliza pushed open the door.

"Good afternoon, Constable." Eliza flashed him a smile. "Is Inspector Adams here?"

"He is, but he's busy at the moment."

"What about Sergeant Cooper?"

The constable smirked at Connie. "I'm afraid he's with the inspector and they don't want to be disturbed."

Eliza's brow creased. "What are they doing?"

Constable Jenkins glanced over both shoulders as he leaned forward and lowered his voice to a whisper. "They've brought Mr King back for questioning."

"Really?" Connie put a hand over her mouth to suppress her squeal, but it was too late to stop Inspector Adams appearing in the reception area to see what the noise was.

"I thought it was you."

"I'm sorry, Inspector." Connie's cheeks flushed. "I didn't mean to disturb you."

The inspector smiled. "As it happens, I'm rather glad you did. We have Mr King in the office and things are about to get interesting."

"Really!" Eliza's eyes widened. "What has he said?"

"Why don't you come through and listen? We've not got to the fine details yet, so you may be able to help."

Mr King was being questioned in a room at the rear of the station and Inspector Adams indicated to two chairs on one side of the narrow corridor. "Make yourselves comfortable, I'll leave the door ajar."

Once seated, Eliza leaned forward in an attempt to see into the room, but her view was restricted to the back of Mr King's head and the profile of Sergeant Cooper as he guarded the door.

"So, Mr King, let me recap." Inspector Adams' voice was clear. "You took the numbered cheques to Mr Hobson so he could fill in your name and the amount to be paid. He then handed them back to you for processing?"

"It's not what it seems."

"What is it then? Why would Mr Hobson so willingly give you half the money he'd recently deposited?"

"The man had more than he needed…"

"And so he decided to share it with his ever so helpful bank manager?"

"Yes! He was sympathetic to the fact I've a wife with expensive tastes."

"But he'd not paid you from his last deposit … had you argued about it? Was he threatening to stop all payments?"

"No, he was going to pay, he just hadn't got around to it."

"Why not? Is there still something you're not telling us?" Inspector Adams paused as he waited for a response. The seconds passed slowly, and Eliza stood up, her mind racing. She had to say something.

"You can't go in." Connie's voice was a whisper.

Eliza peered into the room. "I have to." She pushed on the door, catching Sergeant Cooper's foot as she marched in.

"I suspect it's because he was well aware that the money he was receiving was as a result of theft and he doesn't want to admit it."

Mr King jumped to his feet. "You?"

"Yes, Mr King. I've not heard much of the conversation, but from what I have, I presume the large amounts of money withdrawn from Mr Hobson's account ended up in yours."

Inspector Adams nodded, so Eliza continued.

"I don't believe for one moment Mr Hobson was happy about giving you such a generous amount. Did he want to put an end to your arrangement? Was that why you were so keen to talk to him?"

"He couldn't stop the payments and he knew it..." Mr King spat his words out.

"Was that because you found out he'd stolen the money in the first place and threatened to report him to the authorities if he didn't continue paying you?"

"I would have too."

"But there was a problem, wasn't there?" Inspector Adams paced the edge of the room. "This had been going on for so long, that by reporting him, you'd implicate yourself in the crime. Is that why you killed him to save your reputation?"

"No! I've told you, he was alive when I left him."

"But I'd wager you argued."

"No, it wasn't like that."

Eliza studied Mr King. "If you were going to report him, I imagine he didn't take kindly to it."

"That's all speculation. I didn't kill him, and that's all there is to it."

"All right, then, let's assume you're telling us the truth. By the time you left the maze, it must have been clear that neither of you would come out of the situation with the outcome you wanted. You can't have been happy about that. Perhaps you had an accomplice."

"An accomplice? Why would I...?" Mr King turned away and ran a hand over his hair. "All right, I admit I went there to speak to him about the payments, but that was it. When I left him, I was alone, and he was leaning against the tree in the centre. Sneering at me, if you must know."

Inspector Adams stepped in front of Eliza. "So what happened then? If you'd been in the middle of the maze, you must have passed the killer on your way out?"

Mr King spun back around. "I wish I had so I could give you his name and be done with all this, but I didn't. I wasn't lying when I told you I got lost. Maybe whoever killed Mr Hobson found him while I was stuck in a dead end."

"Either that, or they may have heard the two of you arguing in the maze and slipped in to see Mr Hobson after you left?" Eliza contemplated Mr King as he slumped into a chair.

"It's possible, but I wasn't concentrating. I needed to get back to the family."

Eliza cocked her head to one side. "If you didn't kill Mr Hobson, why were you in such a hurry to leave the palace grounds and return to Moreton?"

"Because..." Mr King groaned "...if I'm being honest, I don't enjoy visiting places like that. We'd only gone because I'd arranged to meet Mr Hobson, and once I was out of the maze, there was no point staying."

"You must have known it would look suspicious."

Mr King's brow furrowed. "Why? I'd gone for a business meeting with a client who was alive when I left him. I'd no idea he was about to be murdered."

Eliza's mouth opened but she momentarily closed it again. "Thank you. Inspector Adams, may I speak to you for a moment?" She indicated for Connie to follow her to the door as she made her way to the reception. Inspector Adams was right behind them.

"What's the matter? Don't you think he did it?"

Eliza shook her head. "No, I don't. I'd certainly say there's a case to arrest him for blackmail, but he's not our murderer. His last sentence was telling. If he'd just murdered a man, he wouldn't have left the trip early and cast suspicion on himself."

Inspector Adams ran a hand over his face. "So what do we do now?"

"I wish I knew. I reckon we can rule out both of our key suspects, but where that leaves us, I've no idea." She let out a deep breath. "I need to think about this."

Connie held out an arm for Eliza to link. "Shall we sit on one of the benches outside? It's a lovely day."

"That sounds like a good idea."

Inspector Adams disappeared back to the office and Mr King, while Eliza led the way over to the seats facing the bowling green. As she sat down, she placed her handbag on the bench and took out her notebook.

"What have we missed?"

Connie sighed. "I've no idea."

Eliza flicked to the beginning of her book. "It all seemed so straightforward when Mr Turner was known to be around the maze and we were searching for the mysterious Mr Swift."

"Are we sure Mr Turner had nothing to do with it?" Connie folded her hands on her lap. "He did give us conflicting information when he came for luncheon."

"He did, but I think Mr King may have helped him out. Mr Turner said he'd heard Mr Hobson and Mr King talking to each other before he left, and now we have proof that they were."

"But we only have his word that he left the maze when he said he did. Perhaps he was the one who waited until Mr King had gone."

Eliza jotted her thoughts into her book. "We'll need to go and speak to him again ... and the other gardeners. I can't help thinking that Mr Clark wasn't in the garden with Mr Turner for as long as he suggested."

"What about the brother? We seem to have forgotten him with all the excitement about Mr King."

"You're right, probably because we've no idea who he is. Inspector Adams was supposed to be looking for him, but I don't know whether he's any further forward. We've made no headway with the murder weapon, either."

"Another reason to revisit the palace, I imagine."

Eliza made a note. "It won't be today though." She stopped writing and stared at Connie. "I've had a thought, could Mrs King help us?"

"How?"

"If Mr King left her alone in the Fountain Garden, you'd imagine she'd be watching out for him. Especially if he was gone for a quarter of an hour or more. If that was the case, she may have seen someone with a knife … assuming the killer walked around the palace and didn't take the shortcut."

Connie shrugged. "I suppose it's worth asking her, although she may not be aware of his arrest yet."

"Hmm. You're right, and Inspector Adams wouldn't be pleased if we took it upon ourselves to tell her."

Connie studied her. "That doesn't usually stop you."

"No, I don't suppose it does, but I get the feeling that even I'd be overstepping the mark if I told her she's unlikely to see her husband for the next few years."

Connie giggled. "You're probably right."

Eliza sighed as she gave her notebook one last glance and put it away. "Come along, let's go home for a cup of tea."

Connie pushed herself up from the bench. "May we call into the shop on the way past? With everything that's been going on this week, I've not managed to bake and I'm out of cake. I could do with buying myself a packet of biscuits."

Eliza grimaced. "If we must. I just hope Mrs Pitt isn't in one of her nosy moods. I'm not sure I can face her this afternoon."

## CHAPTER TWENTY-TWO

The stroll to the shop only took a couple of minutes, but as they approached, Connie stopped and stamped a foot. "For goodness' sake, I'd forgotten! It's Wednesday afternoon, they're closed."

Eliza patted her friend's hand. "Not to worry, we'll go to the surgery for a cup of tea and I'll ask Cook to sort you out with some cake. At least it means we don't have to face Mrs Pitt."

Eliza's stomach sank as her words suddenly sounded hollow in her ears.

"Woo hoo! Over here."

Eliza turned to see Mrs Pitt striding across the village green towards them, a broad grin on her face.

"I was only thinking I'd not seen you for a few days. How's the investigation going? Did I see Mr King being taken to the police station earlier?"

"Mr King?" Eliza's smile froze on her lips. "Oh, yes. He said he had some information that may be useful..."

"Thank goodness that's all it was. Mr Pitt would be furious if we had a murderer living amongst us."

Eliza groaned. "I'm afraid we've hit something of a brick wall on that front. We need to find the victim's brother, but he doesn't seem to be in Molesey."

"Did you say the victim was a Mr Hobson? There shouldn't be too many of them around here."

"The trouble is, they were only half-brothers, and so they have different surnames. Unfortunately, no one knows the brother's name."

Mrs Pitt pushed her hands into her pockets. "That *is* a nuisance. Didn't anyone ever see them together?"

"They weren't on the best of terms." Connie gave the shopkeeper a knowing look.

"Oh, I'm afraid I can't help then."

Eliza smiled. "Never mind, the inspector will have some men working on it. Good day, Mrs Pitt."

She and Connie made to leave, but they hadn't taken more than a couple of steps when Mrs Pitt called them back.

"I remember what I was going to ask you. That man who pushed past us as we waited to go into the palace kitchen. Did anyone speak to him? I got the impression he was racing off to help the police."

Eliza's forehead creased. "I'd forgotten about him. Remind me who he was."

"One of the men who worked at the palace. Or at least I think he did, given the uniform he was wearing."

"What time was this?"

"Ooh, now you're asking. It must have been early, because we were waiting in the alley they call Fish Court."

Recognition crossed Eliza's face. "I remember seeing you

queuing while we were in the Base Court, but if that was when he pushed past you, I doubt he was helping the police. The murder wouldn't have taken place by then, assuming the time of death is accurate."

"Could you give us a description of him?" Connie asked.

"I didn't have a chance to study him, but from what I remember, he was nothing special. I'd say he was average height, average build and had a dark beard."

"It wasn't Mr King, was it?" Connie looked startled, but Mrs Pitt laughed.

"No, although now I think about it, there is a similarity. He was probably around the same age too, but Mr King is taller. No, his only distinguishing feature was his hooked nose."

Eliza's head jerked up from her notes. "A hooked nose?"

"Yes, it was rather distinctive, actually…"

Eliza paused as a shudder ran down her spine, and images from the last few days flashed through her mind. *Oh my goodness.* She stared at Connie. "We need to speak to Inspector Adams. Now."

Constable Jenkins looked up from the desk as Eliza hurried into the police station with Connie close behind her.

"Is Inspector Adams still in the office?"

The constable peered through the door to where Mr King sat in the cell, his head bowed.

"I suppose he must be. Both he and Sergeant Cooper were with Mr King five minutes ago. Would you like me to check for you?"

"No, thank you. We're in a hurry; I know the way."

Leaving Constable Jenkins open-mouthed, Eliza raced to the office where they'd sat no more than half an hour earlier.

Inspector Adams' head shot up as she barged through the door, and he immediately jumped to his feet.

"Mrs Thomson…"

"I know who our killer is."

Sergeant Cooper got to his feet as the inspector gaped at her.

"Won't you take a seat…?"

"There's no time. We need to go to the palace."

"All right, calm down." Inspector Adams strode to the door, closing it behind them. "How do you know, all of a sudden? You were dumbfounded when you left, half an hour ago."

"We bumped into Mrs Pitt."

Incomprehension clouded the inspector's face. "Are you saying she had something to do with it?"

"No, of course not, but thankfully she noticed the murderer while she queued to visit the Great Kitchen. Not that she knew he was the killer, of course." Eliza ignored the seat Sergeant Cooper offered her. "We must go to Molesey and then on to the palace before it closes. If we leave now, we should have time."

"Mrs Thomson, I can't arrest someone without knowing all the evidence."

Eliza stepped to the door and held it open. "You won't have to, I'll explain everything in the carriage. There are a few things we have to confirm, too, before any arrests are made. Firstly, we need to visit Mr Jones and then find Mr Turner. I also want you to check something for me. That's why we need to leave now."

"All in good time, Mrs Thomson." Sergeant Cooper once

again offered Eliza a chair. "Shouldn't you tell Dr Thomson where you're going?"

Eliza glanced at the clock, the corner of her mouth creasing. *Probably, but he'll understand.* "No, he knows we're trying to find a killer."

"Very well, you sit here and I'll ask for the carriage to be brought out. We didn't think we'd need it again today."

Eliza took a deep breath as she bit down on her lip. "Please be quick, Sergeant."

The journey to Molesey was slower than Eliza remembered, and as the horses came to a stop outside Mr Jones' office, Eliza stared at the facade, a knot in her stomach. If the building had seemed closed on the day of their first visit, it looked positively abandoned now. She practically jumped from the steps as the coachman rolled them out.

"Don't tell me that an office with only one deceased client closes on a Wednesday afternoon. He should be open to attract more customers."

Inspector Adams walked in front of her and tried the door. "It's locked."

"That's all we need." She stepped back to study the rooms over the shop. "I wonder if he and his father live up there. Will you bang on the door to see if you can get their attention?"

Sergeant Cooper took over from the inspector and rattled the latch before unclipping his truncheon from his belt. The noise was deafening as he pounded the door, but seconds later a voice shouted from an upstairs window.

"What on earth are you doing? You'll damage the wood."

"Ah, Mr Jones, there you are." Inspector Adams' voice

echoed around the narrow lane. "We'd like a word with you. It would be easier if we could speak inside." He stared at the window until it closed and a minute later, the front door opened.

"What have you done here?" Mr Jones ran a hand over the dented wood and peeling paint.

"It was already like that, sir." Sergeant Cooper inspected the ground as the solicitor glared at him. "May we come in?"

Mr Jones hesitated but he held open the door and ushered them in. "What is it now? I've already told you everything I know."

"We're aware of that, sir, but you may be able to help us." Inspector Adams waited until the door was closed. "We have reason to believe we've uncovered the identity of Mr Hobson's brother, but we'd like you to come to the palace with us to help us confirm it."

"Now?"

"Is that a problem?"

"No, I don't suppose so. I was just in the middle of writing a letter, but it can wait."

"If you wouldn't mind getting your hat and coat then, sir. We're hoping to be there before they close."

As the horse and carriage pulled away from the kerb, Inspector Adams turned to Mr Jones on his left. "Tell us about this new client you have."

"New client?"

"I presume that's why you were writing a letter?"

"Well, yes, but it's not really a client, just some correspondence from a fellow solicitor. Someone who's likely to pay me, which will make a change."

The inspector's eyes narrowed. "Does the work have anything to do with Mr Hobson by any chance?"

"Mr Hobson? What makes you say that?"

"You seem very cagey about it. Has there been a claim against his estate?"

"No ... not a claim exactly, more an enquiry."

"From his brother?"

Mr Jones sighed. "Quite possibly. As I said, the letter came from another solicitor, but they're asking whether there's a will."

"Which solicitor's is this?" Inspector Adams reached up to bang for the attention of the driver. "We should have called on him while we were in Molesey."

Eliza stopped him. "Not now, please, Inspector. We need to be at the palace before it closes. I suspect that having Mr Jones with us will be enough for today, but if not, we can travel back to Molesey tomorrow."

The inspector dropped his arm onto his lap. "Very well. As long as you're sure."

The journey to the palace was mercifully short, and Eliza hurried to get out of the carriage. "Mr Jones, will you escort Mrs Appleton and myself? We'll search for Mr Turner and the other gardeners while Inspector Adams tracks down Mr Marshall. Sergeant Cooper, you're testing out our theory. Are you feeling fit?"

The sergeant inspected his new, slimmer figure. "I wouldn't go so far as to say that, but I'm glad I've shifted a few pounds. Shall I start at the main entrance?"

"Yes, please, and then head for Fish Court and the Great Kitchen. You'll have to find the door that leads to the gardens, but once you do, there should be a path that heads out to the Wilderness. Do you remember the way to the centre of the maze?"

The sergeant flexed his fingers in front of him. "I should be fine as long as I stick to the outer track."

"Splendid. Don't forget, go straight to the centre, wait for a minute and then come straight back out. Once you reach the exit, turn left and move as quickly as you can to the spot where Inspector Adams will be waiting for you. We need to see what time it is when you both meet."

Connie rested an arm on the sergeant's. "I'm sure you'll be fine."

"I will be." His smile had lost some of its sparkle as he focused on his pocket watch. "Right, I make it about half past four. Are we all in agreement?"

"Two minutes past, to be precise." Inspector Adams compared the two watches as they held them side by side. "I'll expect you outside the maze in roughly twelve minutes' time."

Sergeant Cooper took a deep breath. "Very good, sir." On the count of three, he scurried towards the main entrance.

"We'll meet you at the same time." Eliza glanced around the courtyard and the entrance to the gardens. "I hope Mr Turner's still near the walled gardens, we won't find him otherwise."

"At least you have some idea where he'll be. Mr Marshall could be anywhere."

"That's true." Eliza grimaced. "If we can't find everyone within the next fifteen minutes, I suggest we meet up anyway and search for whoever's missing once Sergeant Cooper's finished his test."

Inspector Adams nodded in agreement, and with a final farewell, Eliza took Connie's arm and allowed Mr Jones to lead them through the side gate to the gardens.

"I hope Sergeant Cooper finds his way out of the Great

Kitchen all right." Eliza stared at the side of the palace. "We don't want him delayed because he's got lost."

Connie chuckled. "At least he'll be able to get directions, being in his uniform."

"Yes, he does have an advantage over us when it comes to getting help."

"Not always." Mr Jones scowled. "There are many who don't like the police and will do anything they can to frustrate them. I know from experience when I've needed evidence from them."

"I suppose you're right. Anyway, we'd better get a move on. At this rate, he'll be with Inspector Adams before we are."

They hurried along the row of walled gardens, Mr Jones peering into each one. By the time they reached the third garden, Mr Jones' shoulders were sagging.

"Not a soul, again."

Eliza gave a sympathetic smile. "We've still another couple to try..."

"Look, there he is." Connie pointed ahead of them.

"Oh, what a relief." Eliza raced off, leaving the others to catch her up. "Let's hope Mr Clark and Mr Boyle are with him."

Mr Turner looked up from his pruning as they approached.

"Mrs Thomson. W-what are you doing here?" His eyes flicked between her and Connie but settled on Mr Jones.

"We want you to come with us." Eliza straightened her back, pulling herself up to her full height. "We know who the murderer is."

"It wasn't me!" He jumped back into a newly prepared patch of soil.

"There's no need to panic. Nobody's accusing you." Eliza's eyes swept across the garden. "Are Mr Clark and Mr Boyle around this afternoon?"

Mr Turner eyed them warily. "They should be. Mr Clark was here a few minutes ago, so he can't be far away."

"What about Mr Boyle?"

"I've not seen him since we ate some sandwiches together earlier. He was working in the Wilderness, so he may still be there."

"Very well. Let's find Mr Clark and then we can head over to the maze. We're meeting Inspector Adams in five minutes on the path to the palace; we can search for Mr Boyle on our way."

With a groan, Mr Turner stabbed his fork into the ground. "This soil won't turn itself."

"Maybe not, but neither will a killer hand himself in."

Mr Turner followed them to the footpath. "Are you going to tell me who we're looking for then?"

Eliza shook her head. "Not yet; we need to get everyone together first."

## CHAPTER TWENTY-THREE

Inspector Adams stood part way between the palace and the maze as Eliza approached him.

"Mr Turner; Mr Clark." He raised his hat to the gardeners. "Is there any sign of Mr Boyle?"

"No, not yet. We thought he might be in the Wilderness, but we've not been able to spot him." Eliza scanned the grounds to her left. "Couldn't you find Mr Marshall?"

"I only had time to walk around the Fountain Garden, so he could be on the other side of the palace. Hopefully, he'll walk this way while we're waiting."

Eliza nodded. "I presume Sergeant Cooper hasn't arrived yet."

"No." Inspector Adams took out his pocket watch. "It's one minute after a quarter to five, too. He should be here by now."

Eliza surveyed the path, but there was nothing except a scattering of leaves blowing across the grass.

"Mr Turner, have you seen Mr Boyle yet?"

"I've just remembered–" Mr Clark turned to his colleague

"–didn't he say he was going to work inside the maze this afternoon? There were a few areas that needed repairing."

Mr Turner struck his forehead with his hand. "You're right, he did; I'd completely forgotten." He looked to the inspector. "Shall we go and fetch him?"

The inspector shook his head. "I think it would be better if we all went together."

The lines on Eliza's forehead deepened. "We may need to search the maze too. I'm beginning to wonder if Sergeant Cooper's lost."

The inspector once again studied the pocket watch he'd kept hold of. "You could be right. He should have been here five minutes ago, although if Mr Boyle's in there, he shouldn't be lost. He could have asked him for directions."

"Unless he can't find him."

"That's a possibility, although I'm concerned that there's something else keeping him." The inspector slipped his watch back into his pocket.

"Like what?" Connie's voice squeaked.

The inspector shrugged. "I've no idea, but it's time we went to find out."

Eliza hesitated. "What about Mr Marshall? We need him with us."

Inspector Adams hesitated. "Let's rescue Sergeant Cooper first; we can worry about him later."

Connie gripped Eliza's arm as they walked with the inspector towards the maze. The gardeners and Mr Jones kept in step behind them, but nobody spoke until they reached the entrance.

"Shall we shout him?" Connie's voice was breathless, but the inspector put a finger to his lips.

"No. Let's go quietly so we can hear if anyone's around. It may help if the sergeant's lost in any of the dead ends."

Eliza beckoned Mr Turner, her voice barely a whisper. "Will you lead the way? You're less likely to get lost than us ... and everyone, keep your eyes and ears open for Sergeant Cooper and Mr Boyle."

Eliza and Connie followed Mr Turner in single file, while Inspector Adams brought up the rear behind Mr Clark and Mr Jones. They walked up the left-hand outer wall of the maze and then took several right-hand turns, doubling back on themselves.

Eliza paused at the first opening in the hedge. "This is where we got lost the last time we came. Do you think someone should check the dead ends before we carry on? He may have fallen or something."

Mr Clark agreed to search the two pathways, but within a couple of minutes he returned with a shake of the head. "There's no one down either of them."

"Well, at least we know." Mr Turner continued towards the front of the maze before he once again turned left and headed towards the rear hedge. They hadn't gone far along the path when a noise stopped them.

"Over there." It was the gruff voice of a man. "And keep quiet."

Eliza's mouth dropped open as she faced Inspector Adams. He'd obviously heard the disturbance and pushed past Mr Jones as he peered through the hedge.

"Sergeant, are you in there?" The inspector's voice was clearly audible, but there was no reply.

"That's the middle of the maze." Mr Turner pushed his

face into the hedge. "I'd say there are at least two of them in there."

Inspector Adams indicated for them to follow him in silence until they reached the back hedge. "Which way now?"

Mr Turner scratched his head. "There are several ways, each of which will get you to the centre, but if we take one, whoever is in the middle could leave without being seen."

"We'll need to split up." Mr Clark considered their options. "Perhaps the ladies and Mr Jones should carry on along this path until they get to the next opening." He looked to Mr Turner. "The two of us can then go the longer way around with Inspector Adams. At the junction at the bottom, you come back here, and the inspector and I will take the third path. That way, we'll all end up at the same spot."

Mr Turner nodded. "That would work. It will also mean we've checked all the pathways in case they try to sneak out. Once we meet up and carry on, nobody will be able to leave the centre without us seeing them."

"Splendid." Inspector Adams wiped his brow with a handkerchief. "Mr Jones, if you'll escort the ladies and wait by the next opening, we'll be back as soon as we can."

"I don't like this." Connie's nails dug into Eliza's arm. "What if the murderer's still here and he's got Sergeant Cooper?"

Eliza patted her hand. "Now you're being silly. We know who the murderer is and Sergeant Cooper's perfectly capable of standing up to him."

"I suppose so, but..."

"Look, here's Mr Turner now." Mr Jones pointed down the long stretch of maze. "The others will be here soon enough and we can find out what's happening."

"Precisely. Stop worrying." Eliza squeezed Connie's hand.

Mr Turner kept his voice low when he returned. "There's no one there, so if we carry on we'll meet the others as they come up the next path. Anyone leaving now will have to walk past either us or them."

Inspector Adams and Mr Clark were back within the minute, but the inspector didn't stop.

"There's something going on and we need to get there. Quickly."

Mr Clark continued to lead the way as Mr Turner pushed past the ladies to join the front group. At the far end of the maze, they took the left turn, doubling back on themselves to arrive at the last long stretch of hedge. The inspector and both gardeners disappeared around the corner, but when Eliza and Connie were halfway along the path, they froze.

"Stop. Police." Inspector Adams' voice sounded around the maze as a commotion erupted somewhere to their right.

"What's happening?" Tears filled Connie's eyes.

"I don't know, but it doesn't sound right." Mr Jones raced away before Eliza could collect her thoughts.

"This is no good; we should be with Inspector Adams. Come on." Eliza hitched up the front of her skirt and dashed down the last part of the maze. Connie followed her, but as they rounded the corner, they ran straight into the back of Mr Jones.

"We have to stay here." He blocked the path. "The inspector and the gardeners are dealing with things."

"What sort of things?" Eliza tried to peer around the corner.

"I suspect they need to make an arrest and it won't be safe to go in until they do."

"But…" Connie struggled to push past Mr Jones, but he gripped the top of her arms.

"No buts." Mr Jones peered around the hedge as the shouting from the centre increased. "It's not safe in there."

"But I must see Sergeant Cooper…"

"Mrs Appleton, you need to leave it to the inspector. He'll let you know when it's safe."

"But is Sergeant Cooper all right? I'll never forgive myself if anything happens to him."

"It's not your fault." Eliza's voice was breathy. "If anything, it was mine. I was the one who suggested he make the test run from the palace to the maze."

Mr Jones gave them both a stern look. "It isn't the fault of either of you. You're not the murderer."

Connie yelped. "Has he been murdered?"

"No. At least not that I know of." Mr Jones peered back around the hedge. "What I mean is…"

"I think that's enough, Mr Jones." Eliza put an arm around Connie's shoulders. "Inspector Adams will call us in as soon as he can."

Connie reached for a handkerchief to wipe her eyes, before she clenched her hands together in front of her chest. "We must pray for Sergeant Cooper; Eliza, you need to join me."

Eliza put her hands together, but Connie hadn't spoken more than a sentence when Mr Turner arrived. "Ah, ladies, you're here. Inspector Adams has said you can go through now. He's arrested our murderer."

Eliza's face lit up. "He has?" She grabbed Connie's hand

and pulled her around the final corner and into the centre of the maze. She stopped at the sight of Inspector Adams standing over two men who were sitting back to back, their arms handcuffed around the narrow trunk of the tree. She gazed down at them.

"We were right!" A smile brightened her face, and he returned the gesture.

"Yes, you were."

Connie pulled her hand from Eliza's and hurried to kneel beside Sergeant Cooper, who sat propped up against one of the more sturdy parts of the hedge.

"What's the matter with him?" Connie's voice squeaked.

The inspector wandered over to her. "I'm afraid he's had a nasty bang on the head."

"Oh my goodness." Connie held the sergeant's face as he struggled to focus on her.

"And is this your doing, Mr Marshall?" Eliza glared at the garden attendant.

Inspector Adams answered for him. "Not exactly, but my guess is that Sergeant Cooper stumbled across him when he came into the maze. In his eagerness to help, he tried to arrest him. Unfortunately, he wasn't aware that our killer had an accomplice."

"Mr Boyle." Eliza stared at the second man. "I must admit, I didn't work that out."

"Because I didn't do anything, that's why. It was all him."

"Shut up, you fool." Mr Marshall struggled to free his arms. "I demand to speak to my solicitor."

"Maybe I can help."

Mr Marshall did a double take as Mr Jones stepped forward. "You!"

"Yes, me. Your brother's solicitor."

A smile crossed Eliza's face. "So, we were right about the brother." She studied Mr Marshall. "I presume the fact that you were the one who stabbed Mr Hobson means you hated him as much as he did you."

"You've no proof it was me."

"We may not have seen you plunge the knife in Mr Hobson's back, but we have enough evidence to put you at the scene of the crime, and I'm sure Mr Boyle will help the police with their enquiries."

"He knows nothing." Mr Marshall struggled to see the man sitting behind him.

"So why did you help him?" Eliza glared at Mr Boyle.

"I didn't." There was venom in Mr Boyle's voice. "I saw him going into the maze on the day of Mr Hobson's murder and he told me that if I kept my mouth shut and moved to the far end of the hedge, there was ten pounds in it for me. That's all I did."

A smile flickered on Eliza's lips. "Oh, yes, the small area of hedge next to the footpath that you'd already clipped. That explains how you saw him, but it doesn't explain why you're here now … unless Mr Marshall decided you were an accessory to murder."

"I didn't murder anyone." Mr Boyle's eyes widened.

"No, but the fact you knew Mr Marshall was in the maze when the murder took place, but hid the fact from the police, makes you an accessory. I suspect he used that as a threat to get you to fix the holes in the hedges."

"I only asked him to mend them because they were unsightly. The gardeners should have been on top of it without me pointing it out."

"So it was nothing to do with the fact that once you'd murdered your brother, you slipped through one of these gaps so you appeared to be outside the maze at the time of the death?" Eliza wandered from the centre to the hedge opposite. "This hedge had quite a hole in it last time I was here, but you wouldn't know it now."

"That was the first place he wanted me to mend."

"Because it was the most obvious." Mr Marshall snarled at him. "It was visible as soon as you walked into the maze."

"So once you climbed through, it was only a quick dash to get out again." Eliza paced back to the centre. "I remember when we met you on the footpath to ask the way here, your hat was crooked and you stopped to fix it before speaking to my father. Squeezing through the gap in the hedge would explain it."

"I did no such thing."

Inspector Adams glared at Mr Boyle. "I presume you were in the maze when Sergeant Cooper arrived and tried to arrest Mr Marshall, but why did you hit him over the head?"

"Perhaps he thought the sergeant would stop him getting the money he'd been promised." Eliza raised an eyebrow.

"Could be."

"I didn't hit him hard."

Eliza glanced at Sergeant Cooper, who was still dazed. "Thank the Lord for that."

"You fool." Mr Marshall spat out his words. "Can't you see you're incriminating yourself?"

"No, I'm not, this is all your fault."

"Nobody can prove I was in the maze when the murder took place."

"Actually, I've got a confession to make."

Eliza rounded on Mr Turner, who stared down at his feet.

"I wasn't completely honest with you about the events of that morning."

Eliza took a deep breath. "For goodness' sake, Mr Turner. You've already given us about three different versions of what happened. Were they all lies?"

Mr Turner's cheeks coloured. "No, they were mostly right. I did see Mr Hobson and then Mr Swift arrive at the maze, and I did follow them, but ..."

"But what, Mr Turner?" Inspector Adams' voice growled as he spoke.

"The thing is, when Mr Hobson walked past the gardens, he spotted me working and took great delight in ridiculing me. It was nothing trivial, there was real venom in his voice, and it infuriated me."

"So much so you wanted to kill him?" Eliza's eyes widened.

"I don't know whether I would have, but there was something about the way he strutted to the maze that made me lose my temper. By the time he'd disappeared from view, I was so incensed, I went to the shed and picked up one of our gardening knives. At that point, I had every intention of killing him, but I came out of the shed just as Mr Swift arrived."

"And so you stayed where you were?" Inspector Adams was staring at him now.

"No, I still followed them, because I wanted to see what happened. After about five minutes, Mr Swift left, and so I thought Mr Hobson would be alone. But clearly he wasn't. When I got to the centre, he was already dead."

Eliza glowered at him. "So you didn't turn back as you told us?"

"No, but I couldn't admit to seeing Mr Hobson dead or tell you of my suspicions about Mr Swift, without making myself a suspect."

"That should have been our decision." Inspector Adams' nostrils flared. "If you were innocent, you had nothing to fear."

Mr Turner shook his head. "You knew we had a troubled history…"

"All right, enough." Eliza held up a hand. "If all this is true, why are you telling us now?"

"Because it's occurred to me that I saw Mr Marshall when I was here. I thought nothing of it at the time because he's often around, but…"

"That's lies." Mr Marshall's eyes bored into the gardener. "You're only saying that to save your own skin." He swung his leg to kick Mr Turner, but the gardener jumped out of the way.

"No, it's not. I'd watched Mr Swift leave before I entered the maze, but as I approached the centre, I heard rustling and seconds later noticed Mr Marshall straightening his tunic by the entrance."

"So if he was in here, Mr Marshall couldn't have seen him run across the grass back to his family." Eliza stared at the inspector. "That must have been why Mr King was so adamant there was a mistake, because it was a lie … or at least the bit about being on the grass."

Mr Turner shrugged. "I don't know about that, but it's only just dawned on me that I saw him on the other side of the hedge. Presumably the rustling was him crawling through the gap."

"This is all nonsense, Inspector, arrest him." Mr Marshall struggled with his handcuffs. "He's admitted he brought a knife into the maze to kill my brother, and now he's trying to blame me. You've got the wrong man."

"He didn't bring in a kitchen knife, Mr Marshall. Not like you." Eliza walked to the hedge and back.

Mr Marshall scoffed. "Where would I get a kitchen knife?"

"From the Great Kitchen. Strangely enough, they had one go missing that morning; the one that was later found in the Pond Garden, covered with blood."

"That wasn't me." Mr Marshall's eyes flitted around everyone in the maze. "There's been a mistake."

"There's no mistake." Eliza studied his profile. "Shortly before the knife disappeared, you were seen barging through a crowd of visitors as they queued in the Fish Court."

"You don't know that was me."

"Oh, but I do. We have a witness who told me that the man who so rudely pushed through the crowd wore a palace uniform and had a rather defining Roman nose. I'd say you fit her description perfectly."

"A woman." Mr Marshall spluttered over his words. "You can't convict someone on the basis of anything a woman says."

"I think you'll find we can." Inspector Adams took a step closer to him.

"We also have to consider the fate of the knife." Eliza continued her pacing. "The police have confirmed that the knife recovered in the Pond Garden was the murder weapon. Of all the staff working near the maze that morning, you're the only one who would have had the opportunity to sneak off to a garden on the other side of the palace and dispose of it."

"No, you've got this all wrong. He was my brother. Why would I want him dead?"

Eliza jumped at the sound of Mr Jones' voice.

"Because you'd found out that he'd recently asked me to draw up a last will and testament for him, and guessed you wouldn't be a beneficiary."

"I'd have been more surprised if he'd left me anything. We hadn't spoken for years, and even at Mother's funeral he refused to say a civil word to me. If I'd wanted to kill him, I'd have done it long ago."

"Why would you?" Eliza eyed the attendant. "With no will, you were likely to inherit his money, but once you knew what he was planning, you had to make sure he died intestate. That was the only way to be sure you'd be the sole beneficiary."

Mr Jones nodded. "You even had your solicitor contact me to check that the will hadn't been put in place. Is that how you planned to pay Mr Boyle?"

Mr Boyle glared at Mr Marshall. "He told me I'd be paid as soon as he visited the bank."

"But I presume he failed to tell you he didn't have that sort of money in his account." Eliza raised an eyebrow.

"You cad. I'll get you for this." Mr Boyle shuffled around the tree and kicked out at Mr Marshall, but Inspector Adams stepped in to keep them apart.

"That's enough. I need to get you both out of here." He looked over to Mr Turner and Mr Clark. "Gentlemen, will you help me escort them out? Mrs Thomson, you stay with

Sergeant Cooper until I can arrange for a carriage to collect him."

"No need to worry about me." The sergeant attempted to get to his feet but immediately fell back down.

"Sergeant, sit down." Eliza's voice was gentle. "Mrs Appleton and I will stay with you and take you straight back to Moreton to see Dr Thomson."

Inspector Adams opened Mr Boyle's handcuffs and released him from the tree, as the gardeners blocked the entrance. With the cuffs safely fastened again, Mr Jones held on to the gardener, while the inspector did the same with Mr Marshall. Once they were both free, he and Mr Clark escorted Mr Marshall from the maze, while Mr Turner joined Mr Jones in flanking Mr Boyle.

As soon as they were alone, Eliza leaned over to examine the wound on the back of Sergeant Cooper's head. "That's nasty."

"Will he be all right?"

Eliza's stomach churned. "I hope so."

Connie cradled the sergeant's head as tears flowed down her cheeks. "Please let him get better."

The sergeant relaxed into her embrace, allowing Eliza to get his attention.

"Sergeant Cooper, how many fingers am I holding up?"

His eyes crossed as he squinted at them. "Four."

"No!" Connie wailed as Eliza relaxed the hand that had held up two fingers. "Eliza, can't you do anything?"

Eliza took her friend's hand. "Please try not to worry. He's not in a good way, but he's a strong man, and if we can keep him awake until we get back to Moreton, Archie will be able to sort him out. If you want my opinion, by this time tomorrow, he'll have nothing more than a headache and some dizziness; within a few days, he'll be on the mend."

"But why would Mr Boyle do such a thing?" Connie sobbed into the sergeant's shoulder.

"As with most things in life, it all boiled down to money. As I said, I suspect he feared Mr Marshall wouldn't be able to pay him if Sergeant Cooper arrested him."

Connie ran a hand over the sergeant's head. "That's terrible, he was only doing his job." She held his face close to hers. "Don't you worry, I'll take care of you."

# CHAPTER TWENTY-FOUR

Connie pulled the front door closed behind her as she and Eliza walked from the small house that nestled alongside the police station. They had left Sergeant Cooper sitting in a chair by his fireplace.

"What a relief." Connie exhaled as she paused on the doorstep. "I thought I was going to cry when he correctly stated the number of fingers you held up."

"He'll be fine. Archie gave him a dose of codeine this morning for his headache, and the box I've left will last him the rest of the week. Other than the lump on the back of his head, he'll be as right as rain in no time."

"I do hope so. You won't believe how worried I've been about him."

Eliza smiled. "I have an idea. I've not seen you like this for a long time. You really care for him, don't you?"

There were tears running down Connie's cheeks as she nodded, and she brushed them away with the back of a hand. "What must you think of me?"

"I think it's wonderful. You've found someone to step into Mr Appleton's shoes, and I'm delighted. It's been too long."

Connie giggled. "I feel like a young girl again, but don't go telling anyone."

"As if I would." Eliza grinned. "I'm a model of discretion."

They walked home past the church, but as they approached the shop, Connie stopped. "Do you think we should call in and thank Mrs Pitt for her help?"

"You mean with identifying Mr Marshall? We could do. I don't suppose she's any idea she gave us the final clue."

"No, exactly, but I bet she'll be thrilled to be involved."

Mrs Pitt greeted them with a smile, but the shop door had no sooner closed behind them than it opened again and Mrs Petty joined them.

"Good afternoon, Mrs Petty." Eliza smirked at her. "That was well timed."

The old woman's eyes shone. "I've been following you. I saw you leave the surgery, and when you called at Sergeant Cooper's house, I busied myself in the churchyard until you came back."

Eliza laughed. "There was no need for that, we would have come to visit you too."

"But then Mrs Pitt would have known all about the murderer before me, and I couldn't let that happen." Mrs Petty's sense of fun wasn't lost on Eliza.

"So, do you know who our killer is?" Mrs Pitt leaned forward and rested her arms on the counter.

"We do. And it's all thanks to you."

"Me? I wasn't even near the maze."

"No, but you saw the killer and described him to us perfectly."

Mrs Pitt stared blankly at Eliza. "Who?"

"The man who pushed past you while you waited to go into the Great Kitchen. His name's Mr Marshall, and he's the dead man's half-brother."

"The one with the different name?"

"Exactly. We think he was near the main entrance to the palace when his brother arrived, full of his usual bravado. Mr Marshall saw him heading down the side of the palace towards the gardens and was so incensed that he dashed to the kitchen, bumping into you on the way."

"Why would he do that?"

"He was looking for the biggest knife he could find, with the intention of harming Mr Hobson."

"Gracious." Mrs Pitt put a hand to her chest. "Thank goodness I knew nothing of this at the time. It would have done my nerves no good at all."

Mrs Petty ignored her theatrical neighbour. "Why would he want to kill his brother?"

"Apparently, they hadn't spoken to each other for years, but they both lived in Molesey. If ever they met, Mr Hobson loved to flaunt his wealth and smart clothes in front of Mr Marshall, knowing he could never afford anything like that."

"How mean," Mrs Pitt said. "Why can't people share?"

"From what Mr Marshall said, their animosity stemmed from having to share their mother. Mr Hobson's father died when he was a child, but he was about ten years old when his mother remarried and gave him a brother. Naturally, his young half-brother got more of his mother's affection, but he also had something Mr Hobson didn't have. A father. From the sounds of it, Mr Hobson had resented him for years, and provoking him about his wealth was his way of revenge."

"What a sad tale." Mrs Petty gazed into the distance. "But why kill him a week last Saturday if the feud had been going on for so long?"

"That's an excellent question, and one that took over a week to answer. The thing was, Mr Hobson hadn't written a will. As long as things stayed as they were, Mr Marshall would inherit his brother's money, something that was quite possible given the age difference between them. The problem was, a few weeks before the incident, the two of them had bumped into each other outside Mr Hobson's solicitor's. Unfortunately, Mr Hobson made the mistake of telling his brother he was about to write his will and that he would receive nothing."

"And did Mr Hobson have much money?" Mrs Pitt walked around the counter to join them.

"Oh, yes. More than enough for one man, which meant Mr Marshall stood to lose a fortune. Something he couldn't afford to let happen."

"Mr Hobson was very smartly dressed." Mrs Petty paused. "What did Mr King have to do with all this? He's been arrested, hasn't he?"

"He has." Eliza grimaced. "The thing is, Mr Hobson acquired most of his wealth by illegal means."

"He'd stolen it." Connie spoke with authority as a frown settled on Mrs Pitt's face.

"I still don't see what that has to do with Mr King." Mrs Petty looked to Eliza.

"He was Mr Hobson's bank manager. Somehow he'd found out where the money had come from, but rather than alerting the police to the stolen money, he blackmailed Mr Hobson."

"No!" Mrs Petty's eyes widened. "That would explain why Mrs King always dressed so immaculately.

"And why the furnishings inside the house were so impressive," Connie added.

"Really, are they?" Mrs Pitt took a step closer to Connie. "You've been inside?"

"We have. We found out that Mr King had been near the maze at the time of the murder and so we called in to have a word with him."

"My, you're so brave." Mrs Pitt considered Connie with renewed wonder. "I wouldn't have the nerve to do anything like that."

Connie giggled. "Neither did I; it was Mrs Thomson's idea. I just do as I'm told!"

"No, you do not. You're as good at this as me." Eliza gave Connie an affectionate scowl. "Anyway, seeing inside the house helped us understand why she puts up with him. From what we could see, he's quite a bully."

Mrs Pitt nodded. "Men like that often are. Will he be locked up or transported?"

Eliza shrugged. "We're not sure, but Inspector Adams thinks the judge could jail him for about seven years."

"Well, I hope Mrs King enjoys herself while he's away," Connie said. "In fact, we were going to invite her to the surgery again. She's no reason to turn us down now."

"You're right." Eliza stopped as the shop door opened and Henry joined them.

"I guessed I might find you in here." He smirked at Connie. "How's Sergeant Cooper?"

"Sergeant Cooper?" Mrs Petty exchanged a glance with Mrs Pitt. "Is there something you've not told us?"

Eliza sighed. "Only that Sergeant Cooper accidentally came across Mr Marshall while he was alone in the maze. He already knew Mr Marshall was our killer, so he tried to arrest him, but unfortunately, he didn't know that one of the gardeners was in on the murder. The next thing he knew, he'd been hit over the head with a spade."

Mrs Pitt put a hand over her mouth. "My goodness. Is he all right?"

Connie's eyes teared up again, as Eliza answered. "He will be, but he still has a bit of a headache at the moment." She turned to Henry. "Anyway, why were you looking for us?"

A grin spread across his face. "Father's made arrangements with Cook, and we're having proper afternoon tea together. I reckon he's missed you over these past few days."

"That's nice." Connie smiled. "I expect it will be a farewell tea for Mr Bell too. He goes back to Richmond soon, doesn't he?"

"He does, on Saturday. I feel guilty that I've not spent as much time with him as usual, but it gives me an excuse to visit him in a few weeks' time."

Connie chuckled. "You mean, it will give you an excuse to go shopping with him in London."

Eliza gave her a sideways glance. "I'll be going to visit Henry too. He'll be working by then."

"I won't get there at this rate." Henry made a point of studying his pocket watch. "Are you walking back to the house with me?"

"How can I refuse?" Eliza offered Connie her arm, but her friend shook her head.

"You go and I'll see you later. I'm sure Dr Thomson won't want me in the way."

"Don't talk such nonsense." Eliza walked to the door. "You're as much a part of our family as everyone else, and you were as important to this investigation as me. Not to mention you've had the added worry of Sergeant Cooper. Now, come along. As we said the other day, we do things together, and woe betide any man who tries to stop us!"

## OTHER BOOKS IN THE ELIZA THOMSON INVESTIGATES SERIES

Thank you for reading!
I hope you enjoyed it.

If you'd like details of other books in the series search for
VL McBeath
on Amazon or your local bookstore.

**Other books include:**
*A Deadly Tonic (A Novella)*
*Murder in Moreton*
*Death of an Honourable Gent*
*Dying for a Garden Party*
*A Scottish Fling*
*A Christmas Murder (A Novella)*

**Further books in the *Eliza Thomson Investigates* series are planned for 2023!**

Keep up to date with what's new, by joining my newsletter at:
https://www.subscribepage.com/eti-freeadt
or
visit my website at **www.vlmcbeath.com**

## THE NEXT BOOK IN THE SERIES

### *A Christmas Murder (Novella)*

**A Christmas parlour game, a locked room, and an unlikely death. *Eliza Thomson Investigates…***

*December 1901*: After arriving in Richmond-on-Thames to visit her father, Eliza is surprised to be the guest of honour at a neighbour's Christmas luncheon.

The hostess is keen to hear about Eliza's amateur sleuthing and organises a game of 'Murder in the Dark' to practice her own investigative skills.

But when Connie trips over a body in the drawing room, the victim really is dead … and it looks like murder!

With the killer in the house, tensions are high, but as they wait for the police, Eliza and Connie find themselves in the middle of the accusations.

Can they prove their innocence and get the killer behind bars in time for Christmas?

A Christmas Murder is a novella in the *Eliza Thomson Investigates* series. If you like Miss Marple-style murder mysteries, and women sleuths with attitude, you'll love this historical British series.

Available through my website at:
**www.vlmcbeath.com**/books/eliza-thomson-investigates/a-christmas-murder/

# AUTHOR'S NOTE AND ACKNOWLEDGEMENTS

The idea for having a murder at Hampton Court Palace came from a dinner table discussion with some of the family. I was explaining the location of the fictitious village of Moreton-on-Thames and used the palace as an example of its whereabouts. That quickly led to the suggestion that it could be the site of a murder.

Naturally, the first thing I did was check whether it was actually open to members of the public in 1903. Thankfully, it was.

The last monarch to live in the palace was King George II. He left in 1737, and for years afterwards it became home to an array of aristocrats who were given grace and favour apartments. It wasn't until 1838, a year after her accession to the throne, that Queen Victoria ordered the gates of the palace be 'thrown open to all her subjects' as an early act of generosity.

Even at this early stage, the maze quickly became a major attraction, although until the 1960s it was planted in hornbeam, rather than the visitor-proof yew hedges that form the maze today.

The murder mystery is obviously the central theme of all *Eliza Thomson Investigates* books, but one thing I wanted to address in *The Palace Murder* was the relationship between Connie and Sergeant Cooper. It was a big part of *Dying for a*

*Garden Party*, but when the family went on holiday for *A Scottish Fling*, Sergeant Cooper stayed at home.

As you'll have read, this book brought the two of them closer than they've been in previous books, but will we ever see Connie and Sergeant Cooper get married? At the moment, I've no idea! Part of me worries that it will change the dynamic of her relationship with Eliza, but another part of me would like to see Connie have her 'happy ever after'.

Due to commitments on a new series, there won't be a new *Eliza Thomson Investigates* book in 2021, which gives me plenty of time to think about it. If you'd like to let me know your thoughts, you can message me through my website at: www.vlmcbeath.com/contact

Alternatively, you can keep in touch via my newsletter. To sign up, visit www.vlmcbeath.com

Finally, I would like to thank my friend Rachel, and husband Stuart for their support with this book and for giving early feedback. I would also like to thank those people on my Advanced Review Team who gave me comments prior to the book being available. I really appreciate the help of each and every one of them.

Until next time, take care...
Val

## ALSO BY VL MCBEATH

**Family Sagas Inspired by Family History…**

**The *Ambition & Destiny* Series**

Short Story Prequel: *Condemned by Fate*

Part 1: *Hooks & Eyes*

Part 2: *Less Than Equals*

Part 3: *When Time Runs Out*

Part 4: *Only One Winner*

Part 5: *Different World*

A standalone novel: *The Young Widow*

**The *Windsor Street Family Saga***

Part 1: *The Sailor's Promise*

(*an introductory novella*)

Part 2: *The Wife's Dilemma*

Part 3: *The Stewardess's Journey*

Part 4: *The Captain's Order*

Part 5: *The Companion's Secret*

Part 6: *The Mother's Confession*

Part 7: *The Daughter's Defiance*

To find out more visit: **www.vlmcbeath.com/**

FOLLOW ME

at:

**Website:**
https://valmcbeath.com

**Facebook:**
https://www.facebook.com/VLMcBeath

**BookBub:**
https://www.bookbub.com/authors/vl-mcbeath

Printed in Great Britain
by Amazon